Traci was puzzled by her mother's too-high voice and flushed face. It wasn't like her to interrupt or to treat Mark as if he were a stranger.

"I want to know what's going on," Traci said. "Why can't Mark come to Thanksgiving dinner?"

Mark shook his head. "I think Traci has a right to know," he said softly.

A chill went down Traci's back. Suddenly, she was afraid. "A right to know what?"

I Never Got to Say Good-bye

By Alida E. Young

Cover photo by John Strange

Published by Willowisp Press, Inc.
401 E. Wilson Bridge Road, Worthington, Ohio 43085

Printed in the United States of America

10 9 8 7 6 5 4 3 2

ISBN 0-87406-359-0

For my son, Ben, who gave me so much help with the research for this book.

Special thanks to Phyllis Spechko, RN, C.A.N.P. Research Nurse Practitioner for her expert help and input; to Eileen Upton, RN, M/ED A; and to Chris Hill.

And for their great ideas and help, I'd like to thank the fifth and sixth grade students of Westwood Basics Plus and Santiago Hills Elementary in Irvine, California.

One

"HAPPY Birthday, dear Traci, happy birthday to you."

"Make a wish," Melissa said. Melissa Loring was Traci's best friend.

Traci Crawford closed her eyes and wished. *I wish everything would stay exactly the way it is right now.* She took a deep breath and blew out the fourteen candles on the three-layer cake.

"It's downright unfair," her dad said with a grin. "The older you get, the more candles you have—and the less breath you have to blow them out."

"What did you wish?" Melissa asked.

"Forget the wishes," Jack Lane, one of Traci's friends, said. "When do we eat?"

Mrs. Bagley, the housekeeper, brought in the first of the huge homemade pizzas. While everyone sat on the floor eating, Traci opened

7

the presents from her family and friends. She quickly tore the paper off the large gift from her parents, hoping it was a CD player. It was. And there were several discs packed with it. Her mom and dad always got her the perfect gift.

"Thanks, Mom. Thanks, Dad. It's just what I wanted."

"It should be," her mother said. "You dropped enough hints."

Traci opened the other presents—jewelry and clothes from the girls, and crazy gifts from the guys. She saved Mark's present for last because she knew it would be special.

She picked up the tiny package and looked over at Mark. She was glad he'd made it home from Melrose College. Mark was her uncle, her dad's brother, but he seemed more like her own brother. She and Mark even looked alike. Both of them were tall and slender (Mrs. Bagley called them skinny). And they both had gray eyes and brown hair. Mark was Traci's most favorite person in the entire world.

Inside the small gold box was an antique locket. She clicked it open to find a miniature portrait of her. On the other side was a picture of Mark.

"The locket belonged to Mom," Mark said. "I know she'd have wanted you to have it."

Traci ran over to him. "It's beautiful, Mark. I love it."

"You can take my picture out and put in one of your boyfriend," he said with a wink at all the guys.

Traci gave Mark a hug. As she kissed his cheek, she noticed how hot his skin felt. She looked at him closely. Although the basement party room was nice and cool, sweat dotted his forehead.

"Are you okay?" she whispered.

"I'm fine," he said sharply, too sharply, she thought.

He jumped up. "Let's try out that new CD player. May I have the first dance with the birthday girl?"

Traci's father hooked up the player and put on the music while her mother and Mrs. Bagley brought out more pizza and soft drinks.

The rest of the kids watched, clapping to the beat of the song. Mark had taught Traci to dance, and she knew all the latest moves. As usual, Mark showed off a little.

When the music stopped, the kids applauded loudly. "You two ought to enter a dance contest," Ross Mitchell, a friend of Mark's, told them.

Then Mark went into an old Michael

Jackson routine. Traci stood back to watch. No one would ever guess his right leg had been shattered in a car accident only four years ago, she thought.

Melissa came over to Traci and gave a dreamy sigh. "Mark's so-o-o cute. I wish he was our age."

Traci smiled sympathetically. She knew how it felt to have a crush on an older guy. Last year she'd been in love with Mr. Thompson, her math teacher. And the year before that she'd fallen for a waiter at her parents' restaurant. But now that she was fourteen she thought she was too old for crushes.

The music stopped, and the Brady twins rushed over to Mark, begging him to dance with one of them.

"Would you look at how they throw themselves at him," Melissa said. "It's bad enough to have one of them hanging all over you, but two!"

Traci hid a grin. Melissa was just as bad as Jan and Jenny Brady. Although Mark was six or seven years older than her friends, they all liked him. He'd been a lifeguard and had taught most of the kids to swim.

Traci's mother came over to her. "It looks as if everybody's having a good time," she said. "Your dad and I are going upstairs." She gave

Traci a hug. "Happy birthday, honey."

As soon as her parents left, everybody relaxed a bit more—especially the guys. The kids danced, played Ping-Pong and video games, and managed to eat all the pizzas and two entire layers of cake. Traci danced with all the guys except Ross. He refused to dance with anyone. She liked all of the guys, but none of them was special to her.

At midnight, Traci's dad came downstairs, solemnly carrying a big box of cereal as a hint that they'd better leave before breakfast.

The kids laughed, but they took the hint and started gathering up their jackets. "Everybody who needs a ride, meet me out front," Traci's father said. "Mrs. Crawford and I will drive you home."

"Where's Mark?" Melissa asked. "I wanted to tell him good-bye."

Traci looked around, but Mark wasn't there. "I didn't see him leave. He probably went upstairs for something."

"Great party," everyone said as they left.

"Why don't you have a birthday every Saturday?" Jack asked.

"Sorry. You'll just have to wait until Halloween," Traci told him.

The basement party room was a disaster. But as Traci put away her new discs she smiled happily. The party was wonderful. Life was wonderful. Everything was wonderful.

"Traci," Mrs. Bagley said, "help me clean up this mess."

Well, Traci thought, *maybe everything wasn't wonderful.*

She helped Mrs. Bagley carry glasses and paper plates upstairs. "Have you seen Mark?"

"Not for a while. He must have gone up to bed. He looked tired to me. And skinnier, too." Mrs. Bagley scowled. "I just know that boy doesn't eat right at college."

Mrs. Bagley was a short, plump, grand-motherly type person, but she was as crusty as over-baked pizza dough. At least she pretend-ed to be.

"Thanks for all the extra work you went to," Traci told her. "Everybody loved the pizza, and the cake was super."

"Well, it won't be long before you'll be going off to college and—oh, my stars, I forgot. Mark got a phone message this morning. Something about school tests. I was taking the cake out of the oven, and it just plain slipped my mind."

Traci went over to the kitchen desk and checked the memo pad. The note said he should take his test at nine o'clock on Wednes-day morning. There was a phone number in Melrose with the message.

"I'm going upstairs," Traci said. "I'll put the note in his room."

She said good night to Mrs. Bagley and headed up to her room. She stopped at the large bedroom where Mark stayed when he was home on holidays and summer vacations.

The room was dark, but she knew it as well as she did her own. She'd spent a lot of time there while Mark had been recuperating from the terrible car accident in South America. Her grandparents, Mark's parents, had been killed in the wreck. When Mark was well enough to leave the hospital, he had moved in with Traci's family.

Traci started to drop the note on the desk when she heard a moan. Turning on the desk lamp, she saw Mark lying on top of the bedspread. He was drenched in sweat.

"Mark!"

When he didn't answer, Traci gently shook his shoulder. His skin felt as if he were burning up. "Mark! Wake up!"

He raised up in bed and looked around wildly, as if he didn't know where he was. Then his eyes focused and he saw Traci. "What's wrong?"

"That's what I want to know. You were moaning, and you feel as if you're on fire."

He looked down at the wet covers. "It's

nothing to worry about, squirt. Just a touch of flu, I guess."

"Mom and Dad are taking the kids home. I'll get Mrs. Bagley to call the doctor."

"No! You know how she is about germs. She'll be in here spraying disinfectant. Besides, the doctor will just tell me to take two aspirin and see him in the morning."

"I sure hope you're feeling well enough to take your test tomorrow," Traci said.

"What test?" His tone was guarded.

"There's a message for you that says something about taking a test at school."

"Oh...sure."

Traci handed Mark the note. "Mrs. Bagley forgot to give it to you. That's why I stopped in."

Mark read the note and then crumpled it. "I'm sorry I left your party. I was feeling a little tired."

"Well, if you're sure you're okay, I'd better let you get some sleep." She touched the locket he'd given her. "I love my present. Thanks."

"I'm glad you like it, squirt."

As Traci left the room, she turned back to look at Mark. He was sitting slumped on the edge of the bed, staring at the crumpled sheet of paper.

14

Two

BY the time Traci had gotten up the next morning, Mark had already returned to the dorm in Melrose. He'd left a note saying he felt just fine and not to worry about him. He'd see her at the end of the month at her Halloween party.

Traci hadn't heard from Mark since that note, so a few days before the Halloween party she headed for the kitchen to call and remind him. She had tried three times already, but he hadn't returned any of her calls.

As she started to step into the kitchen, Mrs. Bagley cried, "Stay out! I just mopped the floor!"

The smell of pine disinfectant filled the air. Mrs. Bagley was always worried about germs. She wouldn't even let the dog in the house. She stood with her hands on her wide hips. "You know I always scrub and wax the kitchen floor at four o'clock on Wednesdays."

"I'm sorry. I forgot. I just wanted to call Mark."

"Well, you might as well come in," she relented. Mrs. Bagley always relented if it had anything to do with Mark.

Melrose was thirty miles away, so it was a long-distance call. The guy who answered the dorm phone said Mark wasn't there. "Be sure and tell him Traci called," she said.

During the week, Traci always ate dinner at her parents' restaurant. It was the best place in Weston to eat. At five o'clock Traci told Mrs. Bagley she was leaving, and hurried to the restaurant.

Ordinarily, Traci went in the restaurant through the kitchen, but it had started to rain, so she went in through the front instead. There were only a few people in the main dining room. Waiters and waitresses were scurrying around getting ready for a banquet in one of the large rooms reserved for parties and special occasions. Her mother was at the cash register, going through some papers. "Hi, Mom."

Traci's mother looked up. "Hello, honey. How was school?"

"Okay. I got an A on my algebra test."

"Good for you." Her mother waved toward

the room where the family ate. "Go on back. I'll be with you in a minute."

"Linda? Where's the—" Traci's father stopped as he noticed his daughter. "Hi, honey." He glanced at his watch. "I didn't know it was five already," he said distractedly. "Linda, has the laundry come back? We're going to be out of napkins for the banquet."

Traci knew better than to interrupt during a crisis, even a minor one. She walked past the smaller rooms where groups held luncheon meetings, and headed for the large family room. Some of Mark's paintings decorated the walls of the hall and the little rooms. Traci's father hated modern art, but because the paintings were Mark's and the customers liked them, her dad had kept them on display.

Sometimes it was hard for Traci to think of Mark and her father as brothers. The two were so different. She guessed that was because her father was eighteen years older than Mark.

Traci sat at one of the round tables and poured herself a glass of water. As she waited impatiently, she fiddled with the silverware and practiced making a spoon stay on her nose—one of Mark's tricks.

Finally, she heard someone coming. But instead of her mother, a really cute guy with a tray appeared in the doorway. She recognized him from the high school swim team, but she doubted if he'd know a lowly ninth grader.

"You must be Traci," he said. "Your mom said she'll be here as soon as she can." He set the tray in front of her. "The meatloaf is good, but the carrots..." He made a face. "I brought you some onion rings instead." He grinned and winked. "Just buttering up the boss's daughter."

Traci smiled shyly. "Thanks," she said. "I hate carrots."

"I'm Anthony," he said with a bow. "Busboy, *extraordinaire*." He made a sweeping gesture and knocked over her water glass. As he wiped up the mess, he said, "I guess you can tell I've never done this before."

"You should have seen me the first time I helped out. I dumped spaghetti in the lap of the mayor's wife," Traci said, laughing.

"Anthony?" Traci's father called from the other room.

"I have to go," Anthony said, straightening his black bow tie and pushing back his dark curly hair. "Hope I make it through my first night."

Traci watched Anthony hurry out. She liked him right away. He had a mischievous grin, and his dark eyes sparkled when he laughed.

Traci started eating slowly, expecting her

mother to join her. She was just finishing when she heard a familiar voice. "Hey, squirt, want some company?"

"Mark!" She jumped up, ran to him, and started to give him a big hug.

"No!" her mother said sharply as she came into the room. "Don't get too close. Mark has—a bad case of flu."

"Oh, you know I never get the flu," Traci said and started to give Mark a bear hug.

Mark and Traci's mother exchanged glances, and Mark pulled away. "Your mom's right," he said stiffly. "You don't want to catch my bug."

Traci shrugged. Her mother was getting as bad as Mrs. Bagley when it came to germs. Traci took Mark's hand and drew him to the table. "I tried and tried to get hold of you, but you never answered my calls."

"It's a long story, squirt. I—"

"Mark's been terribly busy," her mother broke in. "You shouldn't bother him at school."

"You are going to feel okay by Saturday, aren't you? You have to be there."

"Well—" Again, he and her mother exchanged looks.

"Mark didn't want to tell you, but he'll be busy that night."

"Busy?" Traci couldn't keep the disappointment out of her voice. "Can't you change your plans? I want you to come."

"Honey," her mother interrupted before Mark could answer. "Mark's getting too old for your parties."

Traci swallowed hard to keep her voice from giving away how badly she felt. "Sure. I understand. The big college guy doesn't want to be seen with high school kids."

Mark started to reach for her hand and then drew back quickly. "Traci, it's not—"

Again, her mother broke in. "Mark, you look starved. I know I am. Let's eat before I have to go back out front."

"I am kind of hungry for a change. I'll go help myself."

"No, no," her mother said. She jumped up, went to the door, and signaled the waiter. "Bring me the meatloaf," she said. "And one New York steak dinner. Medium rare." She turned to Mark. "Just how you like it," she said with a strained smile.

Nobody spoke as they took their seats at the table. Mark broke the silence. "It's not that I don't want to come to your party. It's just that I haven't been feeling so hot," he said. "This—uh—flu—kind of knocked me out the last couple of weeks."

Traci remembered how feverish he'd been the night of her party. He'd said he was better. He did look pale, and Mrs. Bagley was right— he was thinner. "I'm sorry," Traci said. "You should have just said you didn't feel well. So what are you doing here in midweek?"

"Mark, did you hear about Mr. Kellogg?" her mother asked, changing the subject. "He's going to have a triple by-pass. And Mayor Tindall is going to run for the state assembly."

Traci was puzzled by her mother's too-high voice and flushed face. It wasn't like her to interrupt or to treat Mark as if he were a stranger. What was going on?

When her mother finally ran out of local gossip, Traci asked Mark, "Don't you have classes tomorrow?"

"I'm not—"

"Where is Joe with our dinners?" her mother cut in again. She hadn't let Mark finish one sentence or answer anything for himself. She jumped up and went to the door. "Oh, good. Here he comes now."

As soon as the waiter left, Traci asked, "Okay, what's going on?" She looked from one to the other. They just stared at their plates, not eating. "How come you're both acting weird?"

"I'm not going back to school this semester," Mark said bluntly.

"They kicked you out because all the girls can't study when you're around," Traci said, trying to make a joke of it.

He gave her a twisted little smile. "I'm just going to take it easy for a while."

"Great. You can help me with my homework. It'll be so much fun having you home again. Except the house will be full of girls. All my friends have a crush on you."

"Traci, Mark wants to be on his own. Things are different now," her mother cut in, talking too fast. Her voice sounded high and flustered. "Mark, I found a darling apartment not too far from the house."

"I want to know what's going on," Traci said. "Why can't he stay with us like he always does?"

Then she knew what it might be. "Mark! You're getting married. Mom and Dad are upset because you're dropping out of school. That's it, isn't it? Who is she? Vicky? Alyse?"

Mark shook his head. "I think Traci has a right to know," he said softly.

A chill went down Traci's back. Suddenly, she was afraid. "A right to know what?"

Three

"I suppose Traci does have to know," her mother said. "But this isn't the place. We can talk at home—oh, no, we can't. The banquet won't be over until late."

"Mom, *please*," Traci said.

Her mother sighed. "All right, but Alan should be here." She pushed aside her uneaten food. "I'm not hungry, after all. I'll go take care of things out front so Alan can eat something."

"He can have my dinner," Mark said as she hurried out. "I seem to have lost my appetite, too." His voice trailed off into silence.

Traci reached for Mark's hand. "What's going on? Are you in some kind of trouble?"

"I guess you could say that."

Before Traci could ask any more questions, her father hurried in. He set his tray on the table, but didn't sit down. He looked from

Mark to Traci. "Have you told her yet?" he asked.

Mark shook his head. "Linda thought you should be here."

Traci's father sat down heavily, like an old man. Even his face suddenly looked old. Traci was really scared now. She squeezed Mark's hand. "Please tell me what's wrong."

Mark avoided her eyes. "I—uh—" He gave a deep sigh. "I guess there's no way to tell you except straight out. I have a virus called HIV."

"That means human immuno-deficiency virus," Traci's father put in.

"Is that some new kind of flu that—" Traci began. But then she remembered something she'd seen on TV or had read about. "Wait! HIV—that's AIDS!" she cried, and jerked her hand away from Mark's.

"Ssh!" her father whispered. He looked quickly toward the door. "Someone will hear you."

Mark stared down at his hands. Traci saw the hurt on his face. She hated herself for having drawn away from him. But she was still afraid to touch him.

Silence filled the room. Everyone seemed to have stopped breathing. From out front came the clatter of dishes, laughter, someone singing "Happy Birthday."

Traci's father spoke first. "The way the doctor explained it, Mark doesn't have AIDS." His voice was so low Traci had to lean forward to hear him. "But the virus destroys part of the immune system, and Mark's body won't be able to fight off infections and other illnesses."

A little muscle along Mark's jaw twitched as though he were clenching his teeth. "Some authorities think that most people who have the HIV virus will eventually develop AIDS, " he said.

A terrible weight settled in Traci's chest. *Not Mark. Please, God, let it be some awful mistake.* She looked at Mark's face, flushed now. "Are you sure you have this virus—this HIV thing?"

"That's what the doctor claims," Mark said flatly.

"Mark, all the tests came out positive," her father said. "There's no point in denying it."

Traci looked at her father. "How long have you known about this?"

"Just since Monday. I was with Mark when he found out. I know we should have told you. I guess we were all in shock."

"Mark, if you don't have AIDS, why did you quit school?" Traci asked.

"Somehow, word got out," Mark said bit-

25

terly. "I was asked to leave the swim team. My locker was trashed. People were talking behind my back and making jokes about me. Even my best friends asked me if I was gay. My roommate politely told me he wouldn't stay in the same building with me, let alone the same room."

Traci hated to ask her next question, but she had to. "Dad, is that why Mom doesn't want Mark to stay at home?"

"Of course not," her father said quickly, but he avoided Mark's eyes. "If word gets around town, our business could suffer. We can't afford having people stay away from the restaurant because they are scared to death of AIDS."

"Mr. Crawford?"

Traci and her father started guiltily, as if they'd been caught stealing. Traci turned quickly to see Anthony in the doorway.

"Sorry to bother you, sir," Anthony said. "But one of the waitresses is having trouble with a customer."

"Ask Mrs. Crawford to take care of it," her father said impatiently.

"I did, but the guy won't talk to anyone but you. She asked me to come and get you."

Traci wondered how much Anthony had overheard. She couldn't tell by his expression.

Her father jumped up as though he was almost glad to get away from an unpleasant situation. "I'll be back as soon as I can," he said, hurrying out of the room.

After her father left the room, neither Traci nor Mark said anything for a minute. "Mark," she said finally. "You're not gay, and you don't use drugs. How did you get it?"

"You remember all those blood transfusions I had after the accident in South America?"

"Oh, I never thought about the transfusions."

"Well, it was the first thing I thought about when this whole AIDS thing started to get so much attention. I know they can test the blood now, but the tests aren't a hundred percent accurate. And I don't even know if the blood I got was tested."

"You never told me you were worried about getting AIDS."

"Why would I want to worry you, squirt? And besides, I really didn't believe it could happen to me. But then I started getting some of the symptoms I'd read about. I mean, my throat felt as if I'd swallowed broken glass. The lymph glands in my neck and armpits were swollen. I had a fever, and at night I'd sweat so much my bed would be wet."

Traci nodded. "That's the way you were on

the night of my party."

"I really thought it was the flu at first, but I just couldn't get the thought of AIDS out of my head. So I went to see Dr. Adams. That was the test you heard about, not a school test."

"Can't the doctor give you antibiotics or something?" Traci asked.

"No. The virus will stay in my body the rest of my life." Mark's voice was flat and expressionless as if he were talking about someone else. Even if I never get AIDS, I can give the HIV virus to someone else."

I touched him. Involuntarily Traci wiped her hand on her napkin.

Mark gave her a bitter smile. "You can't get it that way," he said. "If I were married, I could give it to my wife. And if she had a baby, the baby would have a good chance of getting it. But you can't get it by touching me."

Traci tried to hide her sigh of relief. "Then I don't see why you can't go back to school if you feel okay."

Mark shrugged. "Because people are scared. There's no cure. If you get AIDS, you die. Even with all the information out about it, people are afraid."

"Mark, are *you* scared?"

He didn't say anything for a second, and

Traci wished she hadn't asked the question. When he answered, his voice was harsh and thick with emotion. "I don't want to die!"

Before Traci could say anything more, her parents returned. But they didn't sit down. "You two had better go to the house now," her mother said. "Mark, the apartment won't be available until the third of November."

"Of course, we'll take care of all your expenses," her father told Mark. "You don't have to worry about a thing—" He stopped. "I'm sorry, Mark. You have plenty to worry about, but not financially."

"You told me not to deny it. Well, You'd better face it, Alan. I don't have insurance, and I sure can't get it now. If I get AIDS, it could cost thousands and thousands of dollars."

Traci's mother glanced at the door and said nervously, "We'd better finish this talk tomorrow. Mark, I don't think you should work here anymore. In fact, it's probably not a good idea for you to be here at all. We can't afford to lose business. Especially now."

"I promise I won't come within a mile of this place," Mark said coldly. "I have some money. I'll get a room at the hotel."

"Now don't be silly. That's not what I meant. We just have to do what's best for everybody. You can stay with us for a few days." Then she looked at Traci. "But I don't want you to breathe a word of this to anyone. Do you understand?"

Traci nodded. She understood the need for not talking about it, but she didn't understand why this awful thing had happened to Mark. The first shock was wearing off now. A knot of fear and anger gripped her stomach, and she felt almost sick. She wanted to scream, *It isn't fair! It just isn't fair!*

Four

TRACI nervously set the articles and pamphlets about AIDS on the checkout desk at the library. She thought Mrs. Bechtel, the librarian, gave her an odd look. *Did she know about Mark?* Traci fumbled for her library card.

"These are for a report," Traci said. "My teacher loads us down with work. I'll never get through all of them. I just hope nobody else chooses this subject." Traci bit her lip, realizing she was babbling.

"It's certainly an important subject," Mrs. Bechtel said. "I hope you get a good grade."

"Thanks," Traci said, and hurriedly jammed the material on AIDS into her book bag.

Traci rushed home, but went inside quietly so Mrs. Bagley wouldn't ask her to do something. Traci felt so helpless. She wanted to read the articles. Maybe knowing more about

31

AIDS would take away the awful empty feeling she had.

As she passed Mark's room, she peeked in and saw him lying on top of the bed. She thought he was asleep, because the room was silent. Mark would have the radio or a cassette playing if he was awake.

In her own room, Traci spread the articles on the bed and began to read them.

She was relieved to confirm that what Mark had told her was right. You couldn't get the virus that caused AIDS from the air or from touching. You couldn't get it from telephones or drinking fountains or shower stalls or toilet seats. You couldn't get it from a person with AIDS if he breathed or sneezed on you. And it wasn't spread by mosquitoes and fleas.

One article told about how the disease was killing men, women, and children in Africa. And it said...*there was no cure.*

A wave of anger flooded Traci. If there was only someone to talk to, someone to tell her everything was going to be all right.

Traci shoved the material into the bottom drawer of her dresser and went to see if Mark was awake yet.

She peeked into the big sunny room. Mark was still lying flat on the bed as if he hadn't moved since she'd last looked in. Stepping in quietly, she saw that he wasn't asleep. His eyes were wide open, and he was just staring at the ceiling. He must have heard her, but he didn't move or say anything.

He probably doesn't want to talk about it, she thought. She hurt for him, but she didn't know what to do or say. An ongoing game of chess was on the card table. During Mark's convalescence after the accident, the two of them had played every game ever invented. His favorite was chess. He said it kept his mind off the pain.

Taking a deep breath, she said brightly, "Hey, Mark, how about finishing our game of chess?"

Without moving his head, he said. "Not today. I'd just like to be alone."

A little stab of pain made her throat too tight to say anything. For the first time in their lives, he had shut her out.

Traci slipped quietly from the room and went directly to the garage where her dog lay curled on his bed. Trixie was actually Mark's pet, but he had given the little terrier to Traci when he went to college.

"Trixie?"

The little terrier jumped up and made a flying leap into Traci's outstretched arms. The dog licked her face. "Oh, Trixie, we have to find some way to help Mark." She buried her face in the dog's fur, and for the first time since she'd heard the awful news, she couldn't keep back the tears.

* * * * *

On Saturday morning, the day of the Halloween party, Melissa came over to help with the decorations and refreshments. While Mrs. Bagley fried homemade doughnuts, Traci and Melissa made fudge brownies.

"How many of these doughnuts do you want me to make?" Mrs. Bagley asked.

"Enough for twelve," Traci said. "I guess three apiece should be enough."

"The Brady twins are on diets, and a couple of the others are into health foods," Melissa said. "Maybe we should fix a tray of vegetables and dip."

"Good idea. I'll see what we have in the refrigerator."

As she wiped the chocolate off her hands, Mark came into the kitchen. "And I'll help," he said. "I'm a whiz at cutting carrot and celery sticks."

"Mark!" Melissa cried, almost dropping the pan of brownies in her excitement. "Traci, you rat, you didn't tell me Mark was home."

Mark had stayed in his room all day Thursday and Friday. He hadn't talked to anyone, and he had hardly eaten a bite in two days. "I—uh, wanted to surprise you," Traci said.

Melissa practically bubbled. "What costume are you going to wear this year?"

"I'm sorry," he said. "I can't come to the party. I have an important appointment tonight. I can help you this morning, though. After I have some breakfast, that is."

Mrs. Bagley mumbled something about not having time to fix a dozen breakfasts.

Mark gave Mrs. Bagley a hug. "I'll just get some cold cereal and a couple of those delicious-looking doughnuts." He gave her one of his big grins that would melt an iceberg.

"You sit down, young man. I'll get you some juice and cereal."

Traci and Melissa grinned at each other. Mark had always been able to work his charm on Mrs. Bagley. As far as she was concerned, he could do no wrong.

When Mark finished eating, he cleaned up his dishes, and then he started looking through the refrigerator for vegetables. "Some of these are a bit wilted, but we can put them in cold water and perk them up. Hand me a knife, will you, Traci."

Traci started to reach into the knife drawer, but then stopped. One of the articles had warned about sharing things that might have blood on them, like razors or toothbrushes. *What would happen if Mark cut his finger on the knife?* "Let Melissa do the vegetables, Mark. I need you to help me carry the soft drinks down to the basement."

Traci hurried to the pantry and pointed to the case of cans. "You get this, and I'll bring the tub for the ice. Keep an eye on the brownies," she said to Melissa on her way back through the kitchen. "They'll be done in fifteen more minutes."

Mark followed Traci downstairs. As he helped her put the cans in the tub, he said, "Don't worry about knives and things, Traci. I'll be careful. You know I'd never do anything that might pass on the virus to you or to anybody else."

"I know. It's just scary."

As they came upstairs, they heard the phone ring. "It's probably Mom," Traci said. "She's been worried about you staying in your room and not eating."

But when they entered the kitchen, Mrs. Bagley held out the receiver to Traci. "It's for you. One of your friends."

"Hi," Traci said. "It's me."

"This is Janice. Sorry to call you so late, Traci, but I can't make it to the party tonight. I—uh—I'm really feeling awful." She coughed. "It's the flu or something, I guess. I don't want to give it to somebody else."

"We'll miss you," Traci said. "But you take care of yourself. Thanks for calling."

"That was Janice Powell," Traci said to Melissa. "She has the flu."

"Now we have an uneven number." Melissa turned to Mark. "Are you sure you can't make—"

The ring of the telephone cut her off. Traci answered it. It was Jack Lane's mother. She said that Jack couldn't make it to the party. He had to be out of town for the weekend.

Traci slowly hung up the phone. "Well, we don't have to worry about having an uneven number. Jack can't make it, either."

"None of the cute guys are coming to the party," Melissa moaned. "You should ask Anthony Delgado. We had dinner at the restaurant last night, and all the girls were dropping their silverware just so he'd have to pick it up."

"Who's Anthony?" Mark wanted to know. "He sounds like a waiter."

Traci felt her face get hot. "Oh, he's just the new busboy Dad hired."

"Just a busboy!" Melissa said. "He's only the cutest guy in the tenth grade. And he's on the swim team and the student council."

Traci was hardly listening to Melissa go on about Anthony. The call from Jack's mother had upset her. A nasty suspicion began to nag her. Jack Lane had never missed one of her parties. And Mrs. Lane had sounded strange.

Melissa chattered on while they worked. The brownies were cooling, and the kitchen cleanup was almost finished when the phone rang again. Traci almost hated to answer it.

This time it was the Brady twins. They both had terrible colds. "The Brady twins can't make it," she said, avoiding Mark's eyes. "They have 'colds.'" She couldn't keep the sarcastic tone out of her voice.

"I don't get it," Melissa said. "I saw them this morning on the way over here. They sure didn't act like they were sick."

Still avoiding Mark's eyes, Traci said, "Maybe somebody else is giving a party, and they'd rather go there."

"Well, I'm going to go find out," Melissa said.

"No!" Traci said sharply, and then said more quietly, "No, don't bother. They aren't worth it. We'll have a better time without them."

Melissa shrugged. "Maybe you're right, but it makes me mad anyway."

"And after I went to all the work of making doughnuts," Mrs. Bagley grumbled.

"I have to get home," Melissa said. "I'll be here right after dinner tonight. Don't worry about those jerks. We'll still have a good time." She looked at Mark. It was easy to see that she had a crush on him. "I hope I see you again before you go back to school."

He nodded. "I'll be here a few days."

After Melissa left, Mark motioned for Traci to follow him into the hall. Once they were out of Mrs. Bagley's hearing, he asked, "Do you think the kids are staying away from your party because they've heard about me?"

"Oh, no," she lied so he wouldn't feel bad. "Everybody at school has a cold. It's going to be a great party."

She tried to sound optimistic, but she wasn't fooling either of them.

At dinner that evening, Traci and Mark both just picked at their food.

"In my day," Mrs. Bagley said, "we cleaned up our plates even if we didn't like the food."

"Dinner's fine, Mrs. Bagley," Traci said. "I just—maybe I'm getting this flu that's going around."

"If you think you're getting sick, you gargle

with mouth wash." Mrs. Bagley jumped up and got a can of spray disinfectant. "Can't be too careful of germs," she said, and began spraying the kitchen. "You two do your bedrooms. Mark, you probably brought some bug home from college."

The phone rang, and Traci hurried to answer it, glad to leave the table.

"It's me," Melissa said. There was a long pause.

"Are you still there?" Traci asked.

"I—I'm here." Then Melissa blurted out, "I'm not coming over tonight."

"What! How come? You're not sick, are you?"

"No, I'm not sick," Melissa said. "I'm upset. I thought I was your best friend."

"Of course, you are. Why are you angry?"

"You know why."

"I swear I don't know what you're talk—" Traci stopped. Were her suspicions right? "Is this about Mark?"

"Why didn't you tell me?" Melissa demaned. "I feel terrible for Mark, but you let me get near him. He has AIDS! I touched the same things he did!"

"Calm down, Melissa. You don't catch it that way."

"You don't know that!"

"I have articles about it. I'll let you read them. Then you'll see."

"I'm not coming near your house. Neither are any of the other kids."

"All right! If you're so stupid, you don't ever have to come over here again. And who was talking about being best friends?" Traci slammed down the phone, so angry she couldn't speak anymore.

"Catch what?" Mrs. Bagley wanted to know.

"It's only right you should know," Mark said. "It wasn't the flu I had. I have the virus that causes AIDS."

Mrs. Bagley turned white, then she backed up until she hit the wall. "AIDS," she said in a hoarse whisper. "Dear Lord above, protect me."

"There's nothing to worry about," Mark said, crossing to her. "To tell you the truth, I think the doctor is wrong. I'm feeling fine now. I'm just a little tired."

Mrs. Bagley just kept shaking her head and rubbing her hands on her apron. "I'm leaving. I'm leaving."

"You can't do that," Mark said. "Who was it who took care of me after the accident? Who helped me with my therapy so I could walk again? Mrs. Bagley, you've been like a mother to me." He tried to put his arm around her as he always did.

She jerked away. "No!" she said.

A flash of hurt and pain crossed Mark's face as if she'd slapped him. "Please listen. I'd never—"

"Just stay away!"

"How can you be so cruel?" Traci yelled at Mrs. Bagley. "You can't catch it by touching him!"

Mark stood there, shoulders slumped. "It's no use, Traci. Everybody's afraid of AIDS. They won't listen to you."

"You're right about that. Melissa acted the same way."

Mrs. Bagley edged her way along the wall until she reached the door. "I just can't stay here. Tell Mrs. Crawford she can send me my check," she said as she rushed out.

The front door slammed.

"Oh, Mark." Traci ran to him and flung her arms around him. "Why don't people understand?"

Five

TRACI helped herself to a celery stick and sat down on a cushion beside Mark. "That's the fifth brownie and the fourth doughnut you've eaten since we came down here," Traci said to him.

"Five doughnuts," Mark corrected her. "Somebody has to eat them up." He rubbed Trixie's ears. With Mrs. Bagley gone, Traci had brought the dog downstairs to the party room.

In the eerie blue light Mark's face looked dejected. He was still hurting over the way Mrs. Bagley had acted.

Traci jumped up and tried to act enthusiastic. "Let's play a game or something."

"I don't—"

The doorbell chimes cut him off. Traci looked at Mark. "Maybe some of the kids are coming, after all."

She hurried upstairs. But when she answered the door, two little goblins held out sacks. "Trick or treat."

Traci got some Halloween candy from the hall table and dropped it in the bags. Then she turned off the upstairs lights so the trick-or-treaters would think no one was home.

She had no more than returned to the basement when the chimes rang again. "I'm not going to answer it," she told Mark.

The chimes kept ringing. "You'd better get it before some kid soaps the windows or toilet-papers the lawn," Mark said.

"I hate Halloween!" she muttered as she stomped upstairs. She grabbed a handful of candy, opened the door, and came face to face with Melissa. She started to close the door.

"Don't go," Melissa said. "I—uh—can I talk to you?"

"Didn't you say enough on the phone?"

Melissa avoided her eyes. "I'm sorry. I shouldn't have yelled at you. It's not your fault if Mark has—"

"It's not his fault, either!" Traci said.

"Traci, don't let this break up your friendship with Melissa."

Traci swung around to find Mark standing in the hall.

"Some friendship," Traci said sullenly.

"Is it true? Mark, do you really have AIDS?" Melissa asked.

"I have the HIV virus that causes AIDS." His voice was even, but Traci could see the tension in his body.

Melissa twisted the belt on her coat. Almost in a whisper, she said, "Traci told me I couldn't catch it by being in the same room with you—or anything like that."

Mark nodded.

"Why didn't you believe me? I don't lie!" Traci said, growing angry all over again.

"A cold is caused by a virus. People catch colds from other people all the time."

"The HIV virus is different," Mark explained. "But if you're uncomfortable being around me, I'll go upstairs."

"No, I believe you." As if her legs were made of wood, Melissa walked stiffly to the door. "I just felt scared, that's all."

"Melissa, how did everybody find out about Mark?" Traci asked.

"Jack Lane said one of the guys on the swim team told him."

"Anthony," Traci mumbled.

"What did you say?" Mark asked.

"Nothing." *Anthony must have overheard them talking at the restaurant,* Traci thought. "But I'll bet I know how the word got out."

Angrily, Traci began yanking down the cardboard skeletons and decorations.

*****

On Monday morning, everybody fixed what they wanted for breakfast.

"Traci, you have to eat something besides doughnuts," her mother said. "I'll call Mrs. Bagley today. Maybe I can get her to come back."

"Can't you find somebody else?" Traci asked. She just couldn't forgive Mrs. Bagley. "The house always smells like disinfectant when she's here."

"She's been with us for years. She'll come back when I tell her that Mark's moving into his own apartment."

Traci's father was reading the morning paper. He slapped it down on the table, nearly tipping over his orange juice. "I don't know why this has to come up right now."

"And I don't know why you always read the editorials every morning," Traci's mother said. "You always get upset. What is it this time?"

"The editorial is against having a group from Melrose open a hospice in Weston for people with AIDS."

"What's a hospice?" Traci wanted to know.

"Is it some kind of a hospital?"

"Sort of," her father said. "It's a program that provides care for people with life-threatening diseases. They're looking for a building or a home they can use to house people with AIDS."

"If you're through with that section, I'd like to read it," Mark said.

Mark took the paper to the counter and spread it out. Traci leaned over his shoulder so she could read the article, too. The editor said he had the greatest sympathy for the victims of AIDS, but it was Melrose's problem, not Weston's. The only case of AIDS he'd heard about in Weston was a student from Melrose College. The editor said that Melrose already had one hospice, so let them open another there if they need two.

"Leonard Backus is against any change," Traci's father said. "And that's the way the town likes it."

The word AIDS in a letter to the editor caught Traci's eyes. The writer said she would fight against any hospice for AIDS patients, just like she'd fought against having those crazies in a halfway house. Let Melrose keep their riffraff, she wrote.

"Riffraff!" Traci exploded. "Sick and retarded people are riffraff?"

47

"Take it easy," Mark said. "It's just one person's opinion. It doesn't mean anything."

The woman went on to say that Weston was known for clean air and clean living, and if she had anything to say about it, Weston would stay that way.

"Well, at least they didn't print my name," Mark said. He wadded the paper and threw it in the waste basket.

Traci's father was writing out a check. "Mark, this morning, you'd better go pay the rest of the first month's rent on the apartment," he said.

"I still have some money in the bank," Mark said.

"No, I want you to take this check."

"All right." Mark reluctantly took the money. "But I'll pay you back as soon as I get a job—if I can get one."

"You might have to go to Melrose to look for a job," Traci's mother said. "Now that everybody in town knows..."

"Yeah, and as soon as my new boss in Melrose would find out, I'd be fired," Mark said bitterly.

"Why don't you try to sell some paintings or your cartoons?" Traci asked. "That way, you could work at home."

Traci's mother nodded in agreement.

"That's a good idea. And the apartment has lots of light."

"I'll take part of tomorrow off and help you move in," her father said.

As Mark folded the check, Traci said, "Wait until after school to pay the rent, and I'll go with you. I want to see the apartment."

"Sure," Mark said. "I'll be housekeeper today and clean up. I noticed the maple leaves need raking out front, too."

"I don't think—" Traci's mother began.

"Don't worry, Linda." Mark crumbled his doughnut in his fist and threw the pieces on the table. "I'll wear my Halloween mask."

"I didn't mean that, Mark," Traci's mother said, her face turning red. "I was just going to say that you should rest," she added lamely.

Traci knew that wasn't what she was going to say at all. She felt the tension in the room. *This is what school will be like today,* she thought. "Mom, I'm not feeling very well," she lied. "Is it okay if I stay home?"

"Honey, I know you're still upset about your friends not showing up for the party, but hiding in your room won't help." Her mother came over to Traci and gave her a little hug. "Maybe it won't be so bad."

"I'm sorry!" Mark shouted. "I'm sorry I'm lousing up all your lives. I'll leave town, and then none of you will have to worry anymore."

"Mark, we're all upset over this," Traci's father said calmly. "It isn't easy for any of us. And yelling at each other isn't going to help."

Traci rushed to Mark's side. She didn't know how he'd managed to control his temper until now. "He has a right to yell. All you care about is what people are saying. All you're worried about is losing customers at the restaurant!"

She had never spoken to her parents like that before, and she expected to be grounded for a month. Her mother started toward Traci, but her father shook his head. "Let her go, Linda. She's just upset."

Almost in tears, Traci grabbed her book bag. "Mark, I'll see you right after school," she said. But she didn't even tell her parents good-bye. She rushed from the room. As she hurried out the front door, she nearly ran into Melissa.

"I thought you might need a friend this morning," Melissa said quietly.

"Boy, do I. I really dread going to school."

"I don't blame you, but we might as well get it over with."

On the way to the high school, neither of them said much. When they started across the campus, Melissa began chattering away about nothing and smiling as if they were having a wonderful time.

As the two of them walked down the hall to their first class, Traci's heart felt as if it were in her throat. Groups of kids stopped talking. They avoided Traci's eyes or turned away. Traci was sure they were talking about her. She held her head high. "My stomach feels like it's full of lead."

"Just ignore them," Melissa whispered.

How do you ignore someone who is ignoring you? Traci wondered bitterly.

She managed to get through her classes, but when she went into the cafeteria at noon, she wished she could just disappear. She straightened her shoulders and tried to ignore the whispers.

As she went through the line, the kids left a wide space in front and back of her. She took only a bowl of soup, hoping it would settle her stomach.

Looking straight ahead, she hurried to an empty table. She sat alone, staring at the soup and tearing her napkin into little pieces. Suddenly she was angry. *Why should I be treated like this?* she wondered. *Why did Mark have to get the dumb disease anyway?* Then she felt ashamed. It was Anthony she should be angry with, not Mark. He was the one who had told everyone about Mark.

Melissa came to the table. "Sorry I'm late."

"You'd better sit somewhere else," Traci told her. "The kids act as if I have AIDS. They might think you've caught it from me."

"Why don't you go to the principal and tell him? Maybe he could have an assembly and explain about AIDS."

Traci shook her head. "People will still be scared. Even my mom and dad haven't touched Mark, and they're adults."

Melissa toyed with her pizza and finally changed the subject. "Do you want to do something after school?" she asked.

"I can't. I'm going with Mark to his new apartment." Traci picked up her tray and uneaten soup. "I think I'll go outside for a few minutes. Maybe the fresh air will help."

"Wait a second, and I'll come with you."

"If you don't mind, I'd like to be alone for a while," Traci said. "But thanks for sticking with me today."

Traci got out of the cafeteria as fast as she could and headed for the back exit. She was standing on the stairs, watching some kids play soccer, but not really seeing them, when Janice came up to her.

"Traci, I—I'm sorry about Mark."

"Sure," Traci said. "And I'm glad to see you

got over the flu so fast," she added sarcastically.

"My mom wouldn't let me come to the party." Janice stared at the ground. "I'm sorry...." Janice looked up and saw the Brady twins headed their way and quickly went back inside.

Janice doesn't want anyone to see her talking to me, Traci thought. The rest of the day no one else spoke to her. The minute classes were over, she grabbed her books and headed for home. Halfway across the campus, she heard someone call her name. She turned to see Anthony running toward her.

Traci waited, anger boiling up inside her.

"I was hoping I'd see you," Anthony said, out of breath. "I'm sure sorry—"

"How could you do it?" she almost shouted.

"How could I do wha—"

Traci cut Anthony off again. "I've never hated anyone before," she cried. "But I do now!" She spun around and took off running.

Six

WHEN Traci arrived home she found Mark packing his books. *He must have a book about every subject in the world,* she thought. It was like having a living encyclopedia around.

He had already stripped the paintings off the walls. Half-filled suitcases lay open on the bed. The fossils Mark had collected were in the waste basket. Traci's anger turned to sadness. The room already seemed empty. "Oh, Mark..."

He looked up. "I didn't know I had so much junk. Unless you want some of it, I'm going to give it to the Salvation Army."

"You can't do that! Not your paintings! And you've been collecting fossils for years."

Mark raised up and straightened his shoulders as if he were in pain. "Are you okay?" Traci asked. She was worried about the grayness of his face and the redness in his eyes.

"I'm just tired." He pushed aside a suitcase and plunked down on the bed.

"You should have waited," Traci said. "I'll help you after we get back from the apartment." She gave him a long look. "Are you sure you should go?"

"I'd better." He got up slowly as if it took every ounce of energy, and put on a jacket. "I move in tomorrow. Let's go, squirt."

As they headed downstairs to the garage, Traci grumbled, "I still think it stinks that you have to move! I don't see why you can't stay here."

"Don't blame your mom and dad. Some people can't handle illness," he said, his voice even. But she could tell how upset he was. Whenever he was angry, his neck turned red.

"How did school go today?" he asked, quickly changing the subject.

The day had been awful, but Mark had enough to worry about. "It wasn't so bad, I guess," she said.

They climbed into Mark's little yellow car. Now it was her turn to change the subject. "Mark, when I'm old enough for a learner's permit, will you teach me how to drive?"

"If I'm still around," he said.

Traci gave him a quick look. *How had he meant that?* she wondered. She wished she could ask him how he felt about having a disease that might kill him, but she figured he wouldn't want to talk about it.

On the way to the apartment, they passed the house where Mark and her dad had grown up. Blackberry vines and hedges that had gone wild nearly hid the place from view. "I wish Alan had been able to sell our old house," Mark said. "I could sure use my share of the money."

"Dad says the land isn't even worth much. This part of town is really run-down."

Mark sighed heavily. "It was a great old house."

Neither said much until Mark pulled into the parking area of the apartment complex, a large two-story building. The grounds had no trees or flowers, no landscaping at all. "It looks like an army barracks," Traci said.

"That's just because it's new." Mark pointed to a large banner across the side that said NOW RENTING. "It probably looks better inside."

They found the manager's office, and Mark rang the bell. A woman came to the door. She gave them a big smile. "May I help you?"

"My sister-in-law, Linda Crawford, put a

deposit on a one-bedroom apartment. She was told it would be ready by tomorrow."

"Oh, yes, I remember Mrs. Crawford. I've eaten at the restaurant many times." The woman sat down in front of a small personal computer and punched in a name. "That's apartment twenty—" She stopped, looked quickly at Mark, then back to the computer. "You—you're Mark Crawford, aren't you?"

"Yes. Is it okay if we take a look at it now? I'll be moving in—"

"Oh, dear, I'm afraid my assistant made an error. That apartment isn't available after all. I'm terribly sorry, Mr. Crawford," the woman said without looking at Mark.

Then the woman jumped up, crossed to a safe, and hurriedly opened it. "I'll refund the deposit right now. I hope you don't mind cash."

"But don't you have another apartment? Your sign says you're now renting."

"Oh, that sign should have come down. We're completely full. I'm so sorry."

Traci and Mark exchanged glances. Mark didn't answer the woman. He just nodded, picked up the money, and jammed the bills into his pocket.

Traci felt hot anger bubbling to the surface. How dare they treat him like this? "I think you're—"

"Come on, Traci." Mark gripped her arm and practically pushed her out the door.

Outside, she glared at him. "Why didn't you let me tell her off? She probably has a dozen vacant apartments."

"I know that, but it wouldn't do any good."

"Aren't there laws against discrimination?"

"Sure, but we can't prove she's lying. Let's get out of here."

Mark's neck was purple-red, and he looked ready to explode. Tracy wished he would let go and not keep all his anger inside. "So what are you going to do?" she asked as they got back in the car.

Mark gripped the steering wheel. "There's no use trying to find an apartment in this town. I'll go over to Melrose tomorrow."

On the way home, Mark slowed down as they passed the big old house. "Do you mind if we stop for a few minutes?" he asked.

Traci shook her head. "The only thing I have to do is homework. Anything is better than that."

Actually, she didn't mind homework all that much, but she knew she couldn't concentrate on it now.

Mark pulled into the driveway, and they got out. A broken FOR SALE sign lay among the tall weeds. Pine needles, turned brown, crackled underfoot as they walked along the path to the big front porch.

In silence, they sat on the steps. As Mark looked around at the place where he grew up, some of the tension seemed to leave him. He leaned back on his elbows and sighed.

"I love this old place," he said wistfully.

"Me, too." Traci looked over at the porch railing and laughed. "Remember when I got my knee caught between the railings? Grandpa had to saw one of the rails off."

"Yeah, and I don't know how many times you fell down the attic steps. I used to think you fell on purpose just so you'd get one of Mom's chocolate-chip cookies."

"I can hardly eat one now without thinking of Grandma." Traci sighed and looked back at the house. "I loved to come here. And you know something? Daddy still comes over here a lot—to clean up the yard and fix the place, he says. He never does though. Mom thinks it's because he doesn't really want anybody to buy it."

"Alan never would admit he's sentimental."

"Would you believe he has the first present you ever made him?"

"Not that old bone I found—the one I thought came from a dinosaur?"

Traci nodded and laughed, then she saw Mark blink rapidly several times. He turned away. "Alan told me he gave the bone to his dog."

"He was teasing you. Daddy's always talking about how you used to follow him around every place."

"Alan called me The Pest, but he let me tag along with him." Mark didn't say anything for a second. His voice was husky as he said, "Alan's been a great brother. After the accident, I don't know what I'd have done without him and Linda—and you, squirt." He reached out and touched her cheek. "I guess you don't realize how much people mean to you until you're not sure how much time you have left."

"Mark, don't talk that way! You sound as if you're going to—die. You said that not everybody with the HIV virus comes down with AIDS. Even if it's ninety-nine percent, you have to think you're the one percent who isn't going to get it!"

"That's not so easy, you know."

"Mark Crawford, after the accident, the doctors said you'd never walk again. You fought back then. You can fight this."

"Okay, okay, I'll try. You're a great little cheerleader, but every time I feel crummy, I think—this is it."

"The government is pouring millions of dollars into research," Traci went on. "We keep reading about new drugs to help. You just have to hang in there until they come up with a cure."

"Sure," he said, sounding unconvinced. He got up slowly and went over to one of the windows. He rubbed it with the sleeve of his jacket and peered in. "Everything looks exactly the way it did before we went on that vacation four years ago."

Traci came up beside him and looked inside. "Except for the dust and cobwebs. Grandma was death on dust. You know, I can almost see Grandpa sitting in the big chair by the fireplace. Mom wanted to sell the furniture, but Daddy wouldn't—"

"Hey, mister! Hey, lady!"

Traci and Mark turned to see a little boy climbing through a hole in the fence. He came up to the steps and stared belligerently at them. "What are you doing here?" he asked as if he owned the place.

Traci tried not to smile. The neighbor boy had probably been using the deserted house as his personal playground.

"Are you going to move in?" he demanded.

Mark looked at Traci. A grin began to spread over his face."Yeah, kid, that's exactly what I'm going to do!"

"Mark, that's a great idea," Traci told him.

"I could fix up the place,'" he said, sounding excited. "It would be a lot cheaper than an apartment."

"And it's close," Traci said, just as excited as he was.

The boy glared at them. Then without a word, he took off, climbing back through the hole in the fence.

Mark ran down the steps and around to the side of the house, with her following. "I can cut down some of these oleander bushes and trim the pine tree. Then my old bedroom would be light enough to paint in."

"I think it's a super idea," she said. "Let's go down to the restaurant and tell Mom and Dad."

The smile disappeared. "Did you forget? I'm not supposed to show my face there."

"Well, it's Monday. They'll get home early tonight. We can ask them then."

Back at the house, Mark said he wanted to lie down a few minutes, and then finish packing.

"I'll call Mom and tell her I'm going to fix dinner for you and me, then I'll come up and help you pack."

"I'd kind of like to be alone for a while. I'm

not hungry, so why don't you go on down to the restaurant and eat."

"Are you sure?" she asked, disappointed.

"I'm sure. I'm feeling a little queasy." He gave her a sickly grin. "Don't look for the rest of the doughnuts and brownies."

"You're sure that's all it is? You're not feeling—you know—crummy?"

"It's AIDS, Traci. Don't be afraid of the word."

"I'm not afraid of the word," she said. "But I am afraid for you."

"I shouldn't have told you about how I feel. Now, you'll be worrying every time I sneeze."

"You'd tell me if you got sick, wouldn't you, Mark?"

He nodded. "I promise."

"Mark, how do you stand it when people look right through you or don't want to be near you?"

"I try to ignore them, but it's hard. I can handle people like that woman at the apartment. But when it's someone like Mrs. Bagley..." He gave her a quick hug. "Thanks for coming with me today."

"And thanks for talking to me—you know—about how you feel and everything."

"Everybody but you avoids the subject. Nobody wants to talk about 'it.' I love you, squirt," Mark said.

Oh, Mark, you're going to be okay. You just have to be.

* * * * *

Traci went in through the restaurant kitchen. Both her mom and dad were busy with customers, so she took her dinner on back to the family room.

She was eating her salad when she heard a knock on the open door. Anthony stood there. "Can I talk to you?" he asked.

"Aren't you supposed to be working?" she asked coldly.

"I'm on my break. Traci, I have to know why you're mad at me. What did I do?"

"You just ruined everything, that's all," she said in a low voice. "You told everybody about my Uncle Mark."

"But I didn't."

"It had to be you. You heard us talking the other day. And Jack Lane heard it from a kid on the swim team. It doesn't take a genius to figure out it was you."

Anthony was shaking his head. "I admit I heard you talking, but I couldn't help it. I sure didn't tell anybody, though. Ross Mitchell's brother Bill is on your uncle's swim team at Melrose College. Bill told Ross, and he spilled it in our locker room. You believe me, don't you?"

Bill Mitchell was a good friend of Mark's—at least he had been. Some friend! Traci stared at her plate, embarrassed that she'd accused Anthony. "I—I thought because you'd overheard..." Her voice trailed off. "I'm sorry."

"That's okay. I saw how the kids were treating you at school. You have a right to be upset."

Traci nodded. "People are so dumb!"

"I know. My grandmother got polio when she was little. She said people wouldn't even come into the same room with her, even when it wasn't catching anymore."

"I'm sorry about your grandmother," Traci said softly.

"Don't feel sorry for her. She's a neat lady. You'll have to meet her some time." He glanced at his watch. "I'd better get back to work." At the door he turned. "If there's anything I can do, just say the word."

"Thanks, Anthony."

Traci felt a warm glow spread over her. The world didn't seem so black anymore. Mark was excited about moving into the house. And she had a new friend. Everything's going to turn out okay, she told herself. It has to!

Seven

"HI, everybody," Traci said to the waiters and kitchen helpers who were eating their dinners before the rush of customers.

George, the cook, looked up at her and laughed. "What happened to you? You look like you've been in a fight."

"I was—with some blackberry bushes." She glanced down at her torn sweater and winced as she touched the scratches on her cheek. "I think I lost."

"I thought your dad had a gardener come in once a week," one of the waiters said.

"Oh, I wasn't working at home. I've been cleaning up around the house that belonged to my grandparents. In four years it's become a regular jungle."

"You finally sold the place?" the cook asked.

"No..." Traci wasn't sure what she should say. Her parents had approved of Mark's using the house. But no one had told her if she was supposed to tell anybody. "I just remembered something," she said quickly. "I'll be back to get my dinner in a minute."

She found her mother changing the flowers in one of the rooms reserved for a party.

"Hello, hon—" her mother began, then stopped as she saw Traci's face. "What in the world did you do to yourself? Are you all right?"

"I was helping Mark at the old house. He was cleaning inside while I tackled the outside. The place is really overgrown."

"You'd better get some disinfectant on those scratches." Then she stopped as if she'd just realized what Traci had said. "You're helping clean up the old place? I told Mark we'd hire someone to do that."

"But he's having fun doing it himself," Traci said. "He says he's feeling great."

"Nevertheless, he shouldn't get overtired. He's susceptible to every bug and virus that comes along."

"That's why I'm helping."

"Traci, I'd rather you stayed away from there as much as possible."

Traci's back stiffened. "You still think we can get it from Mark, don't you?"

Traci's mother busily rearranged the already

arranged flowers. "No, I just think we can't be too careful."

"So, what am I supposed to tell people about Mark living there?"

"It's too small a town to keep it a secret, so it's better if we keep our distance. We've told our customers that Mark doesn't come into the restaurant. So far, business hasn't dropped off, and I want to keep it that way."

Traci wheeled around and headed for the door.

"I'll join you for dinner in a minute," her mother said.

Without turning around, Traci said, 'I'm going home to clean up. I'll fix myself something there."

"Oh, you don't need to. I forgot to tell you—I talked Mrs. Bagley into coming back. She'll stay until we get home. We can talk then, honey."

You can talk until you're hoarse, Traci thought angrily. But I'm not going to desert Mark.

She stopped in the kitchen to tell George not to fix her a tray. As she went out the back she saw Anthony emptying some trash. "Hi," she said absently, still thinking about her mother's attitude.

"Traci, I heard what you were saying about

the bushes and stuff. We have an electric trimmer you can use. It sure makes the work easier."

"Thanks, but I'd probably cut off my fingers."

"I don't work tomorrow. I could come over after school and help."

Traci hesitated. "I don't think you'd really want to. My Uncle Mark's moving into the house."

"So? What difference does it make who's moving in? I'll be there tomorrow after school."

"But—everybody else is afraid..."

"Look," he said. "You need help. I have the tools. I'll be there."

"Thanks, Anthony. We really appreciate it."

She gave him the address. "Hey, I live only a few blocks from there. We're practically neighbors." He put down the lid of the dumpster. "Well, I'd better get back. I can't afford to get fired. See you tomorrow."

He waved, and she watched him hurry inside. Not everybody was afraid. Maybe when people really understood.... She sighed. But how could you make them understand?

*****

70

The minute Traci stepped into the house she knew Mrs. Bagley had returned. The place reeked of pine cleaner.

Mrs. Bagley had always been more like a friend than a housekeeper, but Traci was still angry with her for the way she'd reacted to Mark. She found Mrs. Bagley in the kitchen scouring the counters and cupboards, the phone, anything that Mark might have touched.

If Traci hadn't been so disgusted, she might have been amused at the way the woman looked. She was wearing rubber gloves and a mask. She looked like a surgeon ready to operate.

"Mrs. Bagley, you're being—" Traci started to say ridiculous. She changed it to, "You don't have to be that careful."

"I know what I'm doing, missy," the housekeeper said. Then she sprayed so much disinfectant that both of them coughed.

"I have a bunch of articles upstairs," Traci told Mrs. Bagley. "Doctors and researchers say that the AIDS virus can't live in the air. You'd have to have direct contact with Mark's blood to catch it. The virus would have to get into your blood. Please just read the articles, and you'll see there's nothing to be afraid of."

"That's what you think now, but I remember

when they used to take tonsils out whenever a child had a throat infection. Now, you hardly hear of tonsillectomies. Doctors are always changing their minds, so don't tell me they know everything about it."

"The articles say that if it were easy to catch, nurses who work with AIDS patients and families of AIDS victims would get it. And that hasn't happened."

"I don't care what you say. I'm wearing these gloves and this mask."

Mrs. Bagley began banging cupboard doors. "It doesn't look as if anyone's been to the grocery store since I left. I hope you ate at the restaurant."

"No. I'm going to fix some sandwiches and eat with Mark."

"Well, don't you take any dishes from here!"

Traci bit her tongue so she wouldn't say something. Mrs. Bagley was hopeless.

* * * * *

After school the next day, Traci hurried over to the old house. She found Mark scrubbing window screens. "Hi," he said. "You're just in time to wash windows."

"I don't do windows," Traci said with a smile.

"In that case, I won't invite you to dinner. I have a pot of stew cooking on the stove."

"Then you have electricity," Traci said. "Good. Anthony Delgado's bringing his electric trimmer."

"Anthony's already here." Mark pointed toward the oleander bushes at the side of the house. "Anthony introduced himself. He said he was a friend of yours." Mark winked. "He seems like a nice guy."

Traci blushed slightly. "He is nice," she admitted to Mark. Anthony and Melissa were about the only kids who would even talk to her these days.

Mark handed Traci a bottle of spray cleaner. "You get the downstairs windows, and I'll get the ones upstairs."

Carrying another bottle, Mark climbed up the ladder. "Traci, toss me the paper towels."

Traci found the roll and yelled, "Catch!"

As Mark reached out to grab the flying towels, the ladder tipped sideways. Mark let out a yell.

Anthony rushed to steady the ladder. He grabbed Mark's legs. "Are you okay?" he asked Mark.

"Yeah, I guess. But I'm dizzy."

Anthony held out his hand. "Maybe you'd better come on down."

Mark hesitated for a second. Then he took hold of Anthony's outstretched hand and came down the ladder. "Thanks." He gave a sheepish smile. "I don't know why I suddenly felt so dizzy."

"It's okay, Mark," Traci said. "Anthony knows."

Anthony nodded. "I'm sorry. It must be rough."

Mark shrugged. "It's not so bad. You have to learn to live with it—or die with it," he added.

The statement was like a knife through Traci's heart.

Mark let out a little laugh to take the sting away. "I've been feeling great," he said. "Frankly, I think I was misdiagnosed."

Did he really think that? Traci wondered. Or was he just trying to cover up?

The three of them worked steadily until almost dark. "Who's ready for stew?" Mark asked.

"I'd sure like to stay," Anthony said. "But I have to help my grandmother."

"And Mom will be expecting me at the restaurant," Traci said.

"Why don't you call Linda?" Mark asked. "There's a pay phone at the gas station on the corner."

Traci didn't want to hurt Mark's feelings. "I'd like to stay, but I have homework," she lied.

"Sure. Homework comes first." Mark gave an exaggerated sigh. "And after I slaved all day over a hot stove, as Mom used to say." Then he laughed harshly.

Traci could see Mark's disappointment under the flip remark. "Oh, phooey on homework," she said. "I'll go phone Mom."

"I guess I could come back and eat after I help Grams," Anthony said. "She won't mind."

"Bring her along," Mark said. "I made enough stew for the whole neighborhood."

"Thanks," Anthony said. "But Grams is in a wheelchair. She had polio. She doesn't get out much."

As soon as Anthony left, Traci headed for the phone booth. *I don't care what Mom and Dad say,* she thought as she dropped the coins in the slot. *I'm not going to let Mark eat alone tonight.*

Traci's mother answered the phone. "Mom, it's me. I—"

"Where are you? Are you all right?"

"I'm fine. I just called to ask—"

"When you weren't here at five I called the house. Mrs. Bagley said you didn't come home after school."

"I went over to the old house to help Mark again. Mom, now don't get mad, but I'm going to eat dinner with Mark." Then before her mother could interrupt again, Traci blurted out, "He's fixed dinner—his first company meal, and he wants me to stay. He'll feel awful if I leave now. You didn't say I couldn't come over here—just that you'd rather I didn't, so I'm staying. Is it okay?"

Traci's mother sighed. "I suppose it's all right, but I want you home by eight o'clock."

"I will be. Thanks, Mom."

Traci hung up quickly before her mother could change her mind. As she walked back up the driveway, Traci saw a screaming girl dive through a hole in the fence. Right behind her was the boy Traci had seen the day before. Still screaming hysterically, the girl ran to Traci and hid behind her.

"What's the matter?" Traci asked her. "Are you hurt?"

"Jason spit on me!" the girl howled. "He spit on me!"

Traci hid a smile. "Spitting is a nasty thing to do, but—"

"He spit on me, and now I'll get AIDS!"

Traci knelt down and held the little girl close. "Honey, you can't get AIDS by someone spitting on you."

"Oh, yes, I can!" she cried. "Jason said so. He said I could!"

"Jennifer! Jason! Get back in your yard," a woman yelled from the other side of the fence. "Didn't I tell you both never to go near that house?"

"It's okay," Traci said. "Jennifer just didn't understand. She thinks—"

"Get home you two, before I paddle you both," the woman cut Traci off.

Mark came running up. "What's wrong, Mrs. Wilson?"

"You keep away from my kids, Mark Crawford. We don't want you in our neighborhood!"

Mark's face was a mixture of hurt and anger. "I'm sorry you feel that way, Mrs. Wilson. But this is my home, and I'm staying."

Traci was seething with anger, but lashing out at the woman would only make things worse for Mark.

Mark took a deep breath as if to keep his anger in control. "Mrs. Wilson, I know you're afraid for your kids, but you don't get AIDS from touching someone with the virus. Jason couldn't get it from being near me, and he couldn't give it to Jennifer by spitting on her."

"Well, I heard it's in saliva," the woman said.

"There's never been even one case of AIDS being spread by saliva."

"I don't care what you say. You stay away from my kids!"

Traci and Mark watched the woman stomp down the drive and herd her kids into the house.

Mark just kept shaking his head. "I can't believe it. A five-year-old girl thinks she can get AIDS because her brother spit on her. And Mrs. Wilson thinks I'm going to give it to her kids if I talk to them!"

"Nobody listens when you try to tell them," Traci said glumly.

In the living room, Mark started a fire in the fireplace. His cheerful mood gone now, he and Traci sat on the living room floor, staring at the flames. But even the crackling fire didn't help their moods much.

A knock on the door brought Traci to her feet. It was Anthony with a broad grin on his face. But his smile quickly disappeared when he saw the look on her face.

"What's happened?" he whispered. "Your uncle's okay, isn't he?"

"He's feeling kind of low. He had a run-in with a neighbor. But he's not sick or anything."

Anthony's grin came back. "Good. Because I

have a surprise that ought to make him feel better. "Look what I've brought. Grams made it." He handed a chocolate cake to Traci. "And you can't have a party without people—so guess who's here." He turned and motioned to someone in the shadows.

Ross and Bill Mitchell stepped into the yellow glow of the porch light. They both looked a little embarrassed, especially Mark's friend Bill.

"Hello," Traci said without smiling. She was still angry at them for spreading the news about Mark.

"We ran into Anthony, and he told us Mark had moved into his old house," Bill said.

"So?" Traci said coldly.

"We—uh—we just thought we'd help you celebrate."

"We brought soft drinks," Ross said to Traci. "Is it okay?"

"No, it's not okay. You've practically ruined Mark's life. Thanks to you two even little kids are scared of him!"

Mark came to the door. "Traci, it's all right. The news would have gotten out sooner or later. Come on in out of the cold," he said to the guys.

As they hesitantly went into the living room, Anthony drew Traci aside. "I'm sorry. I thought it would help Mark to know that the guys are really sorry for what they did."

Traci looked at Mark and Bill talking together. "I guess it's all right," she said. "Look, Mark's laughing. You were right to bring them here. Come on, Anthony, let's join the party."

Eight

THE month of November seemed to fly by. Mark was full of frenzied energy, working day and night, finally getting the old place in shape. Traci had helped after school and on weekends. What pleased her the most was that Mark had gone back to his painting and was even talking about going to art school instead of college. He had turned one of the upstairs rooms into a studio, and he'd spent hours working on a painting that no one, not even Traci, had been allowed to see. He planned to enter it in the art fair.

Every year before Thanksgiving, Weston had a pre-Christmas art and craft and food bazaar at the park. It gave people a chance to sell things or to buy handmade gifts for Christmas.

On the morning of the fair, Traci and Anthony planned to meet at the old house.

Mark needed help to take some of his old paintings to sell at the bazaar.

Traci enjoyed the short walk. The day was perfect—crisp, with pale yellow sunshine and air smelling of autumn. On a day like this, she could forget her problems. Most of the kids still avoided her. Nobody ever asked her to baby-sit anymore, but at least Mark hadn't gotten any worse.

As she drew close to the house, she saw Anthony coming from the other direction. They met in front of the gate. "Hi," he said as he held the gate open for her. "It's a great—" He stopped in mid-sentence.

Traci looked up and gasped.

"What kind of creep would do such a thing?" Anthony asked.

Traci stared at the garbage strewn across the lawn—peelings, cans, torn newspapers, broken bottles, even a stained, filthy mattress. "What a mess!"

As they headed toward the house, they kicked aside boxes and trash. Traci saw Mark sitting dejectedly on the front steps.

"Mark? Are you okay?"

He didn't look up. He hit the step with a newspaper, over and over—not hard, not angrily.

Traci sat on the step beside Mark. "Don't

let this get to you," she said. "It was probably some dumb kids."

Mark looked at her as if he'd just realized she was there. "This isn't a kid prank," he said. "This is hate. What are they going to do next? Burn down the house?"

"Mark, it isn't so bad," she said, trying to make him feel better. "What's a little garbage?"

"I think Traci's right," Anthony said. "It was probably some kids trying to be funny. I'll start cleaning up this mess."

Mark stopped hitting the step and held up the tattered newspaper. "I guess neither of you saw the letters to the editor last night."

Anthony took the paper and opened it to the editorial page. "Read the last one," Mark told them.

> *Dear Sir,*
> *We put child molesters behind bars. We jail parents who abuse their children. So how long are we going to let people with AIDS live right next to decent people?*
> *For the good of the community they should be taken away and put some-place where they can't get near our children.*

One of these threats to society lives right next door to me. He is putting my own two innocent children in danger. The police won't do anything. It's up to us, the good people of this community to rid our town of this threat.

The letter was signed by Edith Wilson.

Traci felt half sick. "Oh, Mark, this is awful," she said. "How could the paper print such a horrible letter? Everybody's going to know that Mrs. Wilson's talking about you."

"That woman has always been a trouble-maker in this neighborhood," Anthony said. "Grams says she was always tattling on some-one when she was a little girl—always trying to get somebody into trouble."

"Maybe nobody will pay any attention to her," Traci said.

Mark looked grim as he pointed to the garbage all over the yard. "Somebody already did."

"Let's just try to forget it," Traci said. "Why don't we leave the mess and clean it up later? I want to see that painting you've been working on, Mark. I'll bet you'll win first prize again this year."

"Good idea," Mark said enthusiastically.

"Come on inside."

While they carefully packed the framed paintings for the bazaar, Mark cracked jokes. But his harsh laugh and the look in his eyes gave away the hurt he must have been feeling.

They all squeezed into the front seat of Mark's little yellow car. Trixie sat on her blanket on the backseat.

Anthony started talking about school. He seemed to be trying to take Mark's mind off the letter. "You were student body president when you were a senior, weren't you, Mark?"

"When I was a junior and senior," Mark said. "Why?"

"I'm planning to run for class rep next semester. I just wondered what you did to campaign."

"I found a brilliant girl to be my campaign manager, and we plastered the town with posters and flyers. The first election was just after the accident I was in. Everyone remembered me because I looked pitiful hopping around on crutches."

"Gee, I hate to break a leg just to get elected," Anthony said with a grin. Then he turned to Traci. "But I like the idea of a brilliant female campaign manager. How about it? Want to help me?"

"Oh, I don't know," Traci said, blushing

slightly. "I've never done anything like that before, and I'm pretty busy right now. Why don't you ask Melissa. She's good at organizing, and besides—" Traci had started to say that he'd be better off if he stayed away from her and Mark.

"Why don't you try it," Mark said. "I'll even design the posters and flyers if you want," he said to Anthony.

"You don't have to answer now," Anthony said. "There's plenty of time."

"Where is Melissa, anyway?" Mark asked Traci. "She's not afraid to get near me, too, is she?"

"She had to go visit her grandparents this weekend," Traci said, avoiding Mark's question. Traci knew that Melissa had read the articles about AIDS, but even so, she wasn't sure Melissa really believed it was safe to be around Mark.

By the time they got to the park, the place was already crowded. They set out Mark's paintings and made sure there was a price tag on each one.

"What time does the art exhibit open?" Traci asked.

Mark looked at his watch. "It should be open now."

As they crossed the wet grass to the large

recreation building, some people moved away slightly as they passed Mark. Others avoided looking at him or seemed to look right through him.

"Now I know what a skunk must feel like," Mark said, making an attempt to joke about it. "Probably everybody in town read last night's paper."

"Maybe most of them won't know that you live next door to Mrs. Wilson," Traci said.

A crowd had gathered by the door. A few people spoke to Anthony, but they avoided looking at Mark and Traci.

"Are Alan and Linda going to make it?" Mark asked.

"They have to stop by the restaurant first," Traci said. "They'll be here."

"I hope so. I painted the portrait especially for you and Alan."

Now Traci was more curious than ever to see the painting Mark had been hiding for weeks.

Finally Mrs. Worthy, who ran the art show, came hurrying up. "Sorry I'm late, everyone. We had a flat tire on the way over."

Mrs. Worthy unlocked the door, and the people pushed in. The artwork had been judged the day before, and the paintings had been locked up overnight. "This way," Mark said. "The portraits are in the next room."

Mark led the way through the archway. He stopped so abruptly that Traci ran into him.

"Hey, watch it!" she cried.

Mark swung around. His eyes looked wild. His mouth opened and closed, but no words came out.

"Mark!" Traci grabbed his arm. "What's wrong?"

In a strangled voice, he said, "My painting!"

Traci looked around him and saw a portrait on an easel. A blue ribbon hung from the frame. It was a painting of a girl looking into a mirror. Across the face was a wide gash. Someone had slashed the canvas with a knife.

Rage started in her head and feet and spread inward, meeting in her stomach in a quivering, aching mass. She wanted to strike out at the person who had done this to Mark. Angry tears blinded her for a second. She turned back to Mark just as he took off running.

"Mark! Don't—"

"Let him go," Anthony said softly.

Traci began to cry, and Anthony took her into his arms as if she were a small child. "He needs to be alone for a while."

"Traci? Anthony?"

Traci looked up from Anthony's shoulder to

see her mother and father.

"Honey, what are you crying about? Is it Mark?" her mom asked.

"Is he all right?" her father asked. "We just saw him running toward the river. He didn't even answer us. What happened?"

Anthony pointed to the portrait. "Somebody slashed it."

"Who could have done such a thing?" her mother asked.

Mrs. Worthy came rushing into the room. "Somebody said there'd been some vandalism." She saw the portrait and gasped. "Oh, no! It was the best work Mark's ever done."

"How could this have happened?" Traci asked, still shaking with anger. "This room was supposed to be locked."

"I have no idea," Mrs. Worthy said. "But you can be sure we'll investigate."

As if drawn to the portrait by the cruelness of the destruction, people were just standing looking at it. Traci found herself in front of it, too. Now that she was closer, she saw that the reflection in the mirror looked like her, but the figure was wearing the clothes and hairstyle of a girl in the late thirties. It was her grandmother Crawford. At the base of the mirror were the words, For Alan.

Traci looked up at her father to see him beside her with tears in his eyes. "It's beautiful," he whispered. "Truly beautiful."

"Maybe we should take the painting home now," Traci's mother said to Mrs. Worthy.

"If you don't mind, I think it should stay right here where everyone can see it. Mrs. Crawford, I saw the hateful letter in the paper last night. Not everybody approves of this sort of thing."

Traci's mother nodded. "Thank you."

Traci's father was running his fingers over the gash on the painting. Suddenly he said, "I'm going to find my brother."

* * * * *

On Thanksgiving morning, Traci woke up with a sore throat and the sniffles. Thanksgiving? What did they have to be thankful about this year? Ever since the art show, Mark had seemed to lose interest in everything. A few people had come forward to support him. But the prejudice of others was devastating. Store clerks had refused to wait on Mark when he tried to buy a pair of running shoes. His car had been smeared with black paint.

Traci remembered her birthday wish that everything would stay the way it was that night. Well, nothing was the same. Maybe it was wrong to wish for things.

Today she had to pretend that everything was wonderful because Great Aunt Irma, Uncle Ralph, and three cousins were driving over a hundred miles to join them in a family dinner at the restaurant.

The kitchen had the wonderful aroma of apples and spices instead of Mrs. Bagley's disinfectant. Traci's mother always insisted on baking the pies at home, using an old family recipe.

"I gave Mrs. Bagley the day off," Traci's mother said as she saw Traci enter the kitchen. "Honey, would you peel some more apples for me? Aunt Irma called and said they were bringing four extra people. It's a good thing they won't be staying overnight this year."

Traci took some apples out of the refrigerator and began to peel them. "Mark could put them up at the house. He has plenty of room. What time will they get here?"

Her mother didn't answer for a second. "About noon. They'll go right on over to the restaurant. We'll eat earlier than usual."

"I'd better go tell Mark. I sure wish he'd get a phone put in."

"Uh—Traci—Mark won't be coming to

dinner," her mother said hesitantly.

The paring knife clattered into the sink. Traci swung around. "Why not? Yesterday, he said he was going to wrestle me for the wishbone."

Traci's father looked up from behind his newspaper. "Last night I talked to Mark. We both agreed that it would be better if he didn't join us."

"You let me be with him all the time. Why can't he be with the rest of the family?"

"Of course, we know Mark can't infect them. But Aunt Irma and Uncle Ralph might not understand, and they'd be frightened."

"Why do we have to tell them?" Traci asked.

"If he's there, it wouldn't be fair not to warn—"

"But you just said you know Mark can't infect them. So why do we have to tell them?"

"I'm not going to argue with you, Traci. He's not coming to the restaurant."

"Thanksgiving is a time for families. Mark's your brother, and you asked him to stay away. It's the business you're worried about. You're just afraid somebody will see Mark come into the restaurant!"

"That's enough, Traci," her father said. "Mark understands the situation."

"Well, I don't. If he's not coming to dinner, neither am I. I'd rather starve!"

"You're just being childish," her mother told her. "After the rest of the family leaves, we'll take some dinner over to Mark."

"Leftovers! You treat Trixie better than that! I'm going over to Mark's right now. He's not going to spend Thanksgiving alone."

"You be at the restaurant at one-thirty, or you're grounded for the entire holidays," her father said. "I don't care whether you eat or not, but you're going to be there. Is that understood?"

Traci mumbled, "Yes. But I'd rather eat cold pizza with Mark."

She fled from the room, grabbed her coat, and hurried out. She had to talk to Mark. She had to let him know he wasn't alone.

She practically ran the entire way to Mark's house. Out of breath, she hammered on the door. She could hear Trixie barking inside, so she knew Mark was home. He never left without the dog. Anyway, his car was in the drive. She tried the knob. It was locked.

A little dart of fear sent a chill down her back. When Mark didn't answer, she went around to the back of the house. She tried the door. It was locked, too. Now she could hear Trixie barking in the kitchen. The dog never barked like that. Something was wrong. She peered in through the window of the back door. Mark was lying on the floor. He wasn't moving.

"Mark!"

She beat on the door, but he didn't move. She tried to break the window, but the screen was in the way.

Her heart hammered wildly as she raced to the phone booth on the corner. She dug through her pockets and found some change. In her haste, she dropped a quarter on the floor of the booth. It rolled out into the gravel, and she searched frantically for it.

Finally, she found the coin. She got through to the emergency number immediately, but she was so upset she couldn't think of the house number. "It's on Lancaster Street a block from this phone booth. I remember, I remember, it's 9348 West Lancaster. Oh, hurry, please hurry!"

She found another quarter and called home. "Daddy! Come quick! Something's wrong with Mark. Hurry!"

Nine

THE station wagon skidded to a stop behind Mark's car, and Traci's parents jumped out. "Where is he?" Traci's father asked.

"In the kitchen," Traci said. "I couldn't get in." Traci's mother put her arm around her daughter's shoulder. "Don't worry, honey. Everything's going to be all right."

Why do people always say that? Traci wondered. How can she know if Mark's okay?

Traci's father unlocked the front door with his key, and they all rushed inside. They found Mark lying unconscious on the floor of the kitchen. A stool was tipped over as if he'd been trying to reach something in a high cupboard. Traci's father knelt beside Mark. Traci noticed that her dad hesitated, as if he were afraid to touch Mark.

"Traci, get a blanket," he said. "We

shouldn't move him. He might have a concussion or a broken bone."

All the way upstairs, Traci prayed. *Let Mark be all right, Please let him be all right.*

By the time she got back to the kitchen, Mark was awake and sitting up. "Mark!" she cried. "Are you okay?"

When he tried to answer, he started coughing, a deep, painful sound. He doubled over, holding his chest. Sweat poured down his face, and he lay back down, as if he were too exhausted to hold his head up. "Sorry, squirt."

The paramedics arrived, and Traci's mother seemed to want her to leave the room while they examined Mark.

"Honey, Trixie's whining," she said. "Why don't you go get her and put her in the car?"

Traci found the shivering dog huddled under a table. She picked Trixie up and hugged her. "Mark's going to be okay. He got through that awful car accident. He'll get through this."

As Traci was taking the dog out to the car, an ambulance pulled up in front. She noticed some of the neighbors standing in their yards watching, but no one came over to ask what had happened.

The men from the emergency vehicle stopped to ask directions. Traci led them around the back to the kitchen.

"Could I ride to the hospital with him?" Traci asked her father.

"You go with Mom in the car. I'll have to sign papers and fill out admittance forms. I'll meet you in the waiting room." He patted her cheek. "Mark's going to be all right. We Crawfords are tough."

* * * * *

After rushing to get to the hospital in Melrose, there was nothing to do but wait. "What's taking so long?" Traci asked. "It feels like we've been here for hours."

"I called Mark's doctor as soon as I got here," Traci's father said. "We're lucky he wasn't out of town for Thanksgiv—"

"Oh, good heavens—Thanksgiving dinner," Traci's mother said. "It's too late to call Aunt Irma. They're already on the way."

"While I was waiting for you, I called George and told him we had an emergency," Traci's father said. He looked at his watch. "It's almost noon. I think you and Traci should go on to the restaurant. Tell the family that Mark had a fall."

"But I have to know if he's all right!" Traci cried. "How can anybody eat a big dinner

97

now, at a time like this?"

"Pretend to eat," her mother told her. "Mark wouldn't want Thanksgiving spoiled for the rest of the family."

As Traci and her mother got up to leave, Mark's doctor came out of the emergency room. "Henry, how's he doing?" her father asked.

"Come on back to one of the private offices where we can talk," Dr. Adams said quietly.

When they were all seated in the small room, the doctor removed his glasses and began polishing them. "Mark has a slight concussion," he said, "but the X ray showed no fractures or abnormal swelling."

Traci sank back in her chair, only then realizing how tense she'd been. He was all right.

"However," the doctor went on, "he does have pneumonia. We can't be sure what kind it is until we take further tests."

Pneumonia! All the articles Traci had read mentioned a special kind of rare pneumonia people with AIDS got. Traci's heart sank.

"May I see him now?" Traci asked.

Dr. Adams looked at her closely. "Your nose is a little red. Do you have a cold, Traci?"

"I kind of have a sore throat and the sniffles," Traci said.

"I think it would be better if you waited a couple of days," the doctor said.

A terrible thought struck Traci. "Dr. Adams, could my cold have caused Mark to get pneumonia?"

The doctor shook his head. "No, it's just that Mark doesn't need any complications. His immune system can't fight off infections and viruses as effectively as it should."

"Is it all right if Linda and I go in?" Traci's father asked.

"If you don't stay long. He's quite weak."

"Traci, we'll just be a minute," her mother said. "I'll bring you to visit Mark as soon as your cold is better."

"Tell him I'll save the wishbone," Traci said. "And tell him—" Her voice broke slightly. "Tell him that I love him."

*****

That night, Melissa called. "I'll never eat another turkey drumstick again." Melissa groaned. "Are you as stuffed as I am?"

"Mark's in the hospital," Traci blurted out, without answering Melissa's question. "He has pneumonia."

"Traci, I'm sorry. He's going to be okay, isn't he?"

99

"I don't know. They have to do more tests. Oh, Melissa, I'm so scared for him."

"Why didn't you call me?" Melissa asked.

Traci told Melissa how she'd found Mark. "Then we had to rush back to be with our relatives. It was a terrible day. And I didn't even get to see Mark, because I have a cold."

"Do you want me to come over?"

"Thanks, Melissa, but I think I'll go to bed. Mom says if I get plenty of rest and take some vitamin C, maybe I'll get rid of my sore throat faster."

"Okay. But if there's anything I can do, just call me."

"There's nothing you can do—unless you come up with a magic cure for Mark."

Traci said good-bye and hung up. She felt so helpless. That's what made it so hard. There was nothing she could do for Mark, either.

* * * * *

By Saturday, Traci was over her cold, and it was safe for her to visit Mark. Her mother had some errands in Melrose, so she offered to drop Traci off at the hospital.

"What if Mark's worse? What if they won't let me see him?"

"Honey, your dad saw him yesterday. He was doing just fine. I'll be back in about an hour. Tell Mark that your dad and I will be over tomorrow morning."

Clutching the bouquet of chrysanthemums she'd brought, Traci looked at the grim brick building. She'd been born in this hospital, but she'd never been back. When Mark had his accident, she wasn't allowed to see him.

Traci took the elevator up to the fourth floor and checked at the nurses' station to be sure it was all right for her to visit Mark.

She stood outside his door, putting on a cheerful look. She didn't want him to know how worried she'd been. Expecting to see him hooked up to oxygen and tubes the way she'd seen sick people on TV, she peered in. To her surprise, he was sitting up and playing chess with a boy in the next bed.

"Mark," she said, rushing over to him. "You're okay. You don't even look sick." She gave him a hug, almost smashing the flowers. "Boy, have I missed you."

"I'm fine, squirt." Mark winked at the boy. "She's still the unenthusiastic type."

Mark's voice sounded a little too loud. She looked at him closely. His face was flushed— with excitement or fever—she couldn't tell which.

"Traci, do you remember Danny Walsh?"

Traci looked at the boy in the next bed. "Danny? Danny Walsh from over on Elm Street?"

She would never have recognized him. He was so painfully thin. He looked fragile, as if a stiff wind would blow him over. His great dark eyes with purplish-blue shadows under them seemed too large for his face. She wondered what was wrong with him. "Of course, I remember you. It's good to see you, Danny."

"Don't feel bad, Traci," he said. "Mark didn't recognize me, either."

"Well, it's been a long time since you moved away," Mark said.

"You've changed, Traci," Danny said. "You're not so skinny anymore."

"Skinny! I wasn't skinny!" Traci cried with mock anger. "You always were the rottenest kid I knew, Danny Walsh. Remember when you put worms in my lunch box?"

"You got even, if I remember right. You hid my baseball glove."

Mark looked from one to the other. "I always thought you two were friends."

"Oh, we were," Danny said with a laugh.

"We had a lot of fun. Did you just move back?" Traci asked. "I haven't seen you at school."

"We moved to Melrose a month or so ago," Danny told her.

"Hey, that's great. We'll have to get together."

"Yeah, if I ever get out of this place."

"You two finish your chess game," Traci said. "I'll get these flowers in water, then I can watch you two. Maybe I'll learn something."

"You'll learn something from Danny," Mark told Traci. "I finally found someone who can beat me."

"Don't let him kid you," Danny said. "I can only beat him once in a while. You two visit. I think I'll go pester the nurses."

Danny put on slippers and slowly climbed into the wheelchair on the other side of his bed. "It's great to see you again, Traci."

"Next time I come to visit, I want to hear about what you've been up to since you moved away."

With a wave, Danny wheeled himself out of the room. When he was out of hearing range, Traci asked why Danny was in the hospital. "He looks so thin and weak."

"He has AIDS," Mark said quietly.

"Oh, no! Not Danny. He's so young!"

"Actually, being so young may be in his favor. The doctor said that for some reason young people seem to be able to fight off the disease better than babies or adults."

"Did he get it from a blood transfusion, too?"

"No. His mom died a couple of years ago. After that he started running around with a bad crowd and got into drugs. At a party, he shared a needle with another kid. That kid just happened to have the AIDS virus. One lousy mistake is all it takes."

"I can hardly believe it," Traci said, remembering Danny when they were in grade school. "Danny was full of fun, but he never got into trouble. He still seems like a good kid."

"He is. I've really gotten to know him the last few days."

"I always liked Danny's mother. How did she die? She was just about Mom's age."

"In a fire."

"Oh, that's awful," Traci said. "Was she alone? Where were Danny and his dad? What happened?"

"Apparently the fire started from a faulty heater that Danny's dad had put off fixing. One day, his dad smelled smoke. He woke up his wife and then went to get Danny. They both thought that Danny's mom was right behind him. But she must have gone back to get something. By the time Danny's dad got back to the hall outside the bedroom, the place was an inferno. He couldn't save her."

Traci couldn't say anything for a minute. "Poor Danny. He is just my age...."

"He didn't say so, but I think Danny feels guilty that his dad saved him and not his mom. His dad went to pieces after that. They'd lost everything in the fire and didn't have enough insurance. His dad lost that good job he had. He tried other jobs, but he couldn't manage to hold on to any of them."

"Danny's had a really tough life," Traci said. "How's his dad doing now?"

"I don't know. He hasn't been to see Danny since I've been here."

"But Mr. Walsh was always such a great guy. I remember how he used to let us kids play in his truck and listen to his CB radio. Maybe he has a cold," Traci said, suddenly defensive because she hadn't visited Mark before now.

"Danny and his dad can't seem to talk. Danny makes excuses for his father. He says he's out of town a lot on long hauls. Personally, I think his dad is ashamed that Danny got AIDS from using drugs. Anyway, the kid's lonely. The nurses put me in with him because he doesn't have any visitors."

"I'm glad he was able to talk to you," Traci said. "I hope there's something I can do to help him. I always liked Danny."

Mark reached out and moved one of the chess pieces. "This set of Danny's is missing a piece." He pointed to a safety pin. "That's what we're using for a knight. Traci, if I'm stuck here very long, will you bring over my chess set?"

"Sure, but you look okay to me. Can't you come home now?"

"In a few days. My lungs are still congested, and it feels as if an elephant is sitting on my chest."

"But you're all right, aren't you? I mean you're not—you don't have—you know?" She couldn't say the dreaded word AIDS.

"I don't have pneumocystis carinii pneumonia, PCP they call it, if that's what you're worried about. Thank God for that."

PCP was the kind of pneumonia that people with AIDS get. That was exactly what Traci had been worrying about.

"And the doctor says my helper T cells are okay. Those are the cells that the virus attacks."

Traci nodded. "I've read all those pamphlets you got from the AIDS Project Center." She relaxed. He was still okay.

"Oh, before I forget it," he said, "I finished some posters for Anthony's campaign. They're up in my room. Tell him to choose the one he likes best. He can get copies made."

"It was nice of you to do that, Mark."

Mark had a sheepish look on his face. "There's something else I did. I told Anthony that you and Melissa would work on his campaign."

"Mark I don't want—"

"He was afraid to ask you. I told him you and Melissa couldn't refuse me if I asked."

"You're taking unfair advantage of me," she said. "And you're not even on crutches."

Traci talked with Mark until her hour was up. "Tell Danny good-bye again for me. I'll bring the chess set over tomorrow." She gave him a long hug. "I'll bring an elephant trap, too, so we can get the big guy off your chest."

"Get out of here, squirt," he said with a big smile. But she could tell he was tired.

She turned at the door for one last look. Mark was already lying down, his eyes closed.

Get well, Mark. Please, get well.

* * * * *

The next day Traci took the bus to Melrose so she could spend more time at the hospital. She opened the chess set and looked at the beautifully carved pieces of ivory. Grandma and Grandpa Crawford had bought the set for Mark on the trip to South America. It was one of the few things that had survived the awful car accident. Traci was surprised that Mark still wanted to use it.

When she got to the hospital, Mark and Danny were playing chess.

"Hi, Mark. Hi, Danny. Who's winning?"

"I think I have him on the run," Mark said. "I might even beat him for a change."

"I brought your set," Traci said and put it on Mark's table. As she pulled up a chair to watch, a nurse came in with a wheelchair.

"Sorry to break up your game, Mark, but your doctor wants an X ray." The nurse helped him into a robe.

"Take my place, Traci," Mark said. "But you'd better not lose!"

As soon as Mark left, Traci studied the board for a minute. She looked up and noticed that Danny looked tired. "I'm not really a very good player," she said. "Let's just talk."

"Okay," he said.

Danny leaned back against the pillows. "I was thinking about you last night. Remember the time you got caught up on our roof and couldn't get down? Mom had to...." He stopped. "I guess Mark probably told you about her."

Traci nodded. "Danny, I'm really sorry."

"I miss her." He looked down at his hands. "But I guess I'm glad she doesn't know about me."

"I'm so sorry," she told him again, not knowing what to say.

"Thanks, Traci." Danny sat up in bed and looked at her earnestly. "Maybe it's none of my business, but Mark...." His voice trailed off.

"What about Mark, Danny?"

"Well—I think he's a lot more upset and worried than he lets on," Danny told her.

"I've thought so, too. Sometimes I think he'll erupt like a volcano from hiding his anger."

Danny nodded. "At night he can't sleep. And when he does fall asleep, he has nightmares. Once, I heard him crying."

Traci didn't answer for a minute. When Mark had been recuperating from the accident, everyone had rallied around him. Now, most of his friends were avoiding him.

"I guess I shouldn't have told you," Danny said.

"No, no, I'm glad you did," Traci said. "I thought he'd been handling it pretty well lately. He seemed to enjoy working on the house and his painting."

Danny nodded. "He's hiding his feelings. I

did the same thing when I first found out. My doctor back home did volunteer work for an AIDS Project, and he suggested I go to one of the support groups. It helped me. I told Mark about the Project in Melrose. He didn't want to hear about it."

"What does a support group do?"

"People talk out their feelings. I thought I was the only one who was scared, and it helped to know I wasn't the only one with problems. Anyway, I just thought you might be able to get Mark to go to one of the groups."

"Thanks, Danny," Traci said slowly. "I'll see what I can do."

"The Project has all sorts of classes and counselors. And they have a buddy system— you know, one person helps another. As soon as I get out of here, I'm going to see if I can be a buddy."

"When do you think you'll go home?" Traci asked.

"Oh, I can't go home." He stopped as if he wished he hadn't brought up the subject. "The doctor says I can't stay alone."

"But I thought Melrose Hospice would send a nurse to your place."

"Nobody would come there. We live on the third floor of our building. There's no elevator or hot water. It's just temporary until

Dad gets back on his feet."

If Danny needed that much help, how did he plan to be a buddy to someone? Traci wondered. He was the one who needed someone to look after him.

"Can't you go into a nursing home?" she asked.

He shook his head. "Nobody will take people with AIDS," he said flatly. Then he gave her a smile that lit up his face. "How about finishing that chess game?"

"Sure," Traci said. "Or do you want to start a new one on Mark's set?"

He picked up the safety pin. "I like this old one, even if the knight is missing. But if you'd rather—"

"No, this is fine," she assured him.

"Dad bought me this set the Christmas we moved away from Weston. He still owned his truck then, and sometimes he'd talk Mom into letting me go on short hauls. I'd ride up in the sleeper behind Dad and pretend I was driving. I've always wanted to be a trucker."

Traci remembered that was all Danny had ever talked about. He leaned back against the pillows again and closed his eyes. He seemed to have forgotten the chess game, even forgotten she was in the room.

"I used to love to listen to the calls on the

111

CB radio," he went on. "Everybody used weird names to identify themselves. My handle is Squeaker. That's my dad's nickname for me."

"I know," she said softly.

Danny opened his eyes and looked at Traci. "I didn't mean to go on about myself this way."

"I'm glad you did."

Suddenly, Mark came bursting into the room as if his wheelchair were a rocket. "I'm going home tomorrow!" he yelled. "Traci, tell that brother of mine that I need a ride at ten in the morning."

Mark got out of the chair and plopped down on his bed. "Whew, I guess I don't have as much strength as I thought." He stretched out on the bed. "Well, did you finish the game?"

"No," Danny said. "I've been talking too much." Then his face saddened. "It's sure going to be quiet in here after you leave."

"Hey, I'll be over to see you Danny-O."

"Me, too," Traci told him.

"You don't have to do that," Danny said. "Anyway, I'm going to be up and around pretty soon."

Danny looked so frail and thin. He tried to put on a brave front, but Traci didn't think he would ever be up and around on his own.

"We'll be over to visit," Mark said firmly. "Never argue with a Crawford. We're too stubborn."

Traci glanced at her watch. "I'd better get going. Melissa and I are going over campaign strategies with Anthony tonight. He said to tell you thanks for the poster. He chose the red, orange, and yellow poster—the one with the caricature of him."

Traci gave Mark a quick hug. "I'm so glad you're coming home." Then she turned to Danny. "I hope you'll get to go home soon."

But would he? He looked too sick to go anywhere. Would he ever go home again? Traci quickly pushed that terrible thought out of her mind.

Ten

WHEN Traci arrived at the Delgado house for the campaign meeting, Melissa and Anthony already had the posters and flyers laid out on the kitchen table. This was the first time she'd ever been in Anthony's house, and she looked curiously around. The small house was cluttered with medical equipment, but it was spotlessly clean.

"Mom's working at the hospital," Anthony said. "And Grams is resting. She'll be out to meet you in a little while."

"How's Mark?" Melissa asked, as they sat around the table.

"I'm really worried about him. I keep wondering—is this it? And I know he worries about it, too. He hardly ever smiles anymore."

Traci didn't know what she'd do without Melissa and Anthony. They were the only ones she could talk to. She couldn't let Mark know how she felt. And her mother and father didn't want to even discuss the subject.

Traci slapped the table. "Enough of my problems. Let's get busy."

"Did either of you think of any places to put the flyers?" Anthony asked.

"What about at car washes and supermarkets?" Traci asked.

"No good," Anthony said. "The flyers would just get thrown away. We need a place where kids hang out."

Traci found it hard to be enthusiastic. School campaigns seemed so unimportant compared to Mark's problems.

The three of them were still discussing ideas when Anthony's grandmother wheeled herself into the room. Anthony jumped up. "Grams, I want you to meet my friends."

He introduced everybody. Mrs. Evans, Anthony's maternal grandmother, was a tiny woman. She was pretty and had a young-looking face. One of her legs was withered and much thinner than the other.

Mrs. Evans rolled her chair close and reached out to touch Traci's hand. "How's your young uncle doing?"

"I told Grams," Anthony said quickly. "But she's the only one. Even my mom doesn't know."

"It's okay," Traci said. "I'm not so sure how Mark's doing, Mrs. Evans. He isn't getting his strength back. One minute he's moping around. The next, he's making plans and acting as if he thinks the doctor is wrong."

"Oh, I remember those feelings when the doctor said I had polio. I felt as if I were on a roller coaster. But sometimes denial is important. It may be helping Mark get ready to face what might be ahead for him."

Mrs. Evans squeezed Traci's hand gently. "My dear, just give him lots of love. Try to keep a positive attitude—for you and for him."

"Grams would be bedridden if she weren't so optimistic," Anthony said. "You should see all she does around here."

"I don't know how you were able to bake that beautiful cake for Mark," Traci said.

"Cooking's not so hard. Until recently, I got around with just a walker." Mrs. Evans pointed to the four-legged aluminum frame that would support her when she walked. "But for some reason I'm losing power in my muscles again."

"They call it post-polio syndrome," Anthony explained. "After all this time it doesn't seem fair that she has to get worse again."

"Well, it didn't get me down forty years ago, and it won't stop me now," his grandmother said briskly. "By the way, how is the campaign coming? I really like the poster your uncle made for Anthony. It's simple and eye-catching. Your uncle's very talented."

"I agree," Melissa said. "The poster's great. We had a bunch of flyers made from it, but we haven't figured any good way to distribute them yet."

"When I was a girl, I ran for student body president. I got permission from the principal to go into the classrooms early. I put a flyer on every desk."

"Did it work?" Traci asked.

"Well, I was president for two years."

"That sounds like a good idea to me," Melissa said. "I'll check with Mr. Grayson and see if we can get permission."

Traci glanced at her watch. "I have to go now." She turned to Anthony's grandmother. "I'm really glad I got to meet you."

Just talking to Anthony's grandmother had made Traci feel better. No wonder Anthony understands about Mark, she thought.

* * * * *

"Mark, do you feel like going to see Danny today?" Traci asked.

"Sure. I'll drive."

"Should we take a game?" she asked. "Something the three of us can play?"

"Bring the Scrabble set. Danny's good at word games."

When they got to the hospital, they stopped at the nurses' station to see if they could go in. Mark spoke to the nurse who had attended him.

"Oh, I'm sorry," the nurse said. "Danny's gone to a hospice—Sunrise House." She gave Mark the address. "It's not too far from here. I'm sure he'll be glad to see you two."

They found the location with no difficulty. Mark pulled up in front of an old house that was badly in need of paint.

Inside, a woman at a desk in what would have been the dining room, led them to Danny's room on the second floor.

There were two hospital beds in the bare room. Danny was sitting huddled in a rocking chair by the window. The afternoon sun streamed over his gaunt face. He looked even thinner than before. His face lit up when he saw them.

"Hi," he said. "It's great to see you two." He motioned toward two straight chairs. "It feels good here in the sun." He lowered his voice and grinned at Traci. "I think they're trying to save money on heat."

Traci had started to take off her coat because the room was too warm, but she left it on. "How do they treat you here?"

"Fine. They aren't always sticking needles in me and taking tests."

Traci nodded toward the other bed. "I hope you have a better roommate than Mark," she said with a laugh.

"My roommate died last night," Danny said flatly. "He'd been in a lot of pain. People were in and out of here all night helping him. I—I didn't get much sleep."

"Maybe you'd rather we came back some other time," Mark said.

"No, no. It's pretty boring here alone." He gave them a weak smile. "It really is great to see you."

Traci felt ill at ease. She wanted to leave, but Danny seemed so glad to have company.

"We brought a Scrabble set," Mark said. "Do you feel like playing?"

"Let's just talk for a while. If you don't mind, though, I think I'll get into bed."

Climbing slowly out of the rocker, Danny looked like an old man. He seemed unsteady on his feet, and his shoulders hunched forward as he crossed to the bed. Even in the terry cloth bathrobe, Traci could see how wasted his body looked. The material seemed too heavy for his thin shoulders.

Oh, Danny, you're so young. Traci fought to keep her lips from trembling.

When Danny had settled down in the bed, Mark and Traci pulled their chairs up close. "How are you doing, Danny-O?" Mark asked.

"If you really want to know—not so great."

"Do you feel like talking about it?" Mark asked.

"My stomach hurts something awful. And I have diarrhea a lot." He glanced over at the empty bed. "I guess I'm lucky, though."

Lucky! Lucky! Traci thought.

"I'm doing better, here," Danny went on. "I'm planning to go with my dad on his next long haul."

"That's great that he's been to visit," Traci said.

"Oh, sure. He brought me here and everything."

Mark had said he thought Mr. Walsh was ashamed of Danny. I'll bet he hasn't been back to visit since, Traci thought angrily.

"He's in Arkansas right now," Danny said, frowning. "Or maybe it's Kentucky. I can't remember."

The three of them talked for a while longer. Traci remembered what Mrs. Evans had said, and tried to sound optimistic. But it was hard. Danny's eyes kept closing. Mark and Traci exchanged glances.

"Hey, Danny-O, we have to get home," Mark said. "We'll come back in a few days."

"Is there anything special we can bring?" Traci asked. "Ice cream? Magazines?"

Danny shook his head. "No, I'll be out of here in a few days. But I'll give you a call when I get back from the trip with my dad. Maybe we can go to a movie or something."

"That—that would be fun," Traci said, swallowing hard. She reached out and gently squeezed Danny's hand. "We'll do lots of things."

Mark and Traci hurried from the room. She managed to get clear outside before she burst into tears. "Oh, Mark, doesn't he know how sick he is?"

"He knows. He knows." Mark put his arm around her and held her.

"How much time do you think he has left?"

Mark just shook his head.

Time. She had never realized just how precious it was. She wished she could gather up all the minutes and hours she'd ever wasted and give them to Danny.

Mark swore under his breath. "This lousy disease! How many more of us is it going to get before there's a cure!"

Through her tears, Traci looked up at Mark's strong, handsome face. In a few months or years, would he look wasted and sick like Danny?

Please, don't let Mark get sick. Please, don't let him die!

Eleven

THAT night Traci and her father ate dinner in the family room at the restaurant. Traci was just moving the spaghetti around on her plate.

"Honey, you haven't eaten two bites," her father said. "What's bothering you?"

"I can't get Danny out of my mind. He's so sick, Dad."

"I don't think you should go over to the hospice. It just upsets you," her father said.

"But he doesn't have anybody but Mark and me."

"Where is his family?" he asked.

"I told you his mom died. And his dad just never comes to visit Danny. He's always on the road in his truck, Danny says."

"Maybe it's hard for him to see his son dying," Traci's father said, pushing his plate aside and almost knocking over his glass of water. He didn't say anything for a long while, then he almost spit out the words, "Not everybody can be around sick people. It doesn't mean they don't care."

He stared off into space. "When your grandmother had cancer, I couldn't even go near her. I was scared because she had that awful disease. Mama would expect me to kiss her good night, but I couldn't go close to the bed. I just couldn't!"

"Cancer isn't contagious," Traci said. "Why were you afraid?"

"I don't know. I wasn't thinking about it. I was only feeling. But I did care." His voice broke. "I really did care."

Was he talking about Grandma Crawford—or about Mark? Traci wondered.

Her father cleared his throat and gave an embarrassed little laugh. He didn't often let people see his feelings. "Well," he said, briskly getting to his feet. "I'd better get to work before this place falls apart."

"But, Dad, is it okay if I visit Danny? I think it really helps him to have somebody to talk to."

Her father hesitated, and Traci thought he was going to say no. "All right. But I don't want to see you so upset anymore that you can't eat your meals."

Traci picked up her fork and forced down a bite of cold spaghetti. "I'll eat. I promise."

* * * * *

The next Saturday when Traci went to see Mark, she found him lying on the couch listening to music. Trixie was asleep beside him.

"Hi," she said brightly. "Want to go ice skating today?"

He just shook his head.

"How about a game of chess? Or Scrabble or Monopoly?"

"I don't feel like playing games," he said irritably.

Traci didn't either, but she hated to see Mark so down. "Can I fix you something to eat? Do you need your laundry done?"

"Traci, stop hovering over me. Don't try to be so darned helpful."

"I'm sorry," she said, knowing he didn't mean to hurt her feelings. "Have you heard anything from the art school?" He'd been anxious to start next month.

"No. But it doesn't make any difference. The whole thing's a waste of time. It takes too many years to become a good painter."

"Mark, you're only twenty-one. You're already a wonderful artist. I'll bet you'll be famous by the time you're thirty. I'll brag to everybody, 'That's my uncle.' "

"Oh, stop it!" he said harshly. "You and I both know I'm going to look just like Danny soon."

"Mark Crawford, don't you dare talk like that! You said that your immune system is still okay. Maybe you were right—maybe the doctor misdiagnosed you."

"I was kidding myself. I just didn't want to admit it."

Traci remembered what Danny had said about the AIDS Project. "Maybe you should talk to someone." She told him about the Project.

"Thanks, but I don't need to be around a lot of sick people. And I don't need somebody telling me how lucky I am. Or telling me that I could be lots worse off."

"I just thought it might help...."

"Look, Traci, I know you're trying to cheer me up, but I don't feel much like talking. Okay?"

"Sure," she said. She was getting used to his up and down moods. "Is there anything I can do for you while I'm here?"

"You can feed Trixie. She's probably hungry."

Traci took the dog to the back porch, filled

her food dish, and made sure she had water. On her way out, she called, "I'll see you."

"Traci, come back." Mark hurried to the door to catch her. "I'm sorry, squirt. I shouldn't take my rotten mood out on you."

"I don't mind. Honest."

He put his arms around her. "How did I get so lucky to have a niece like you?" His voice got all raggedy. Traci looked up at him.

"Mark, what's wrong?"

"I went back to the doctor for a checkup. My T helper cells have gone from 400 down to 160."

"What does that mean?"

"It means—" He took a deep breath and blew it out slowly. "It means that my immune system is rapidly failing. The doctor says I'm becoming susceptible to all sorts of things— bacteria, parasites, viruses, other diseases— that normally would have little or no effect on me."

"Oh, Mark, no!"

"I didn't intend to tell anybody, but—"

"Well, I'm glad you did," Traci said. "Are you going to tell Mom and Dad?"

"Not yet. Don't worry."

But she did worry. She'd read enough about AIDS to know this was serious.

* * * * *

Traci visited Danny as often as possible. They played games when he had the strength. Mostly they talked about the fun times they'd had. It seemed to help him to talk to people he used to know.

After school one day near the middle of December, Traci took a bus to the hospice. The day was cold and gray, the kind of gray that usually meant snow was on its way. Already, the streets of Melrose were brightly decorated for Christmas. A radio was softly playing "Silent Night."

Christmas. Traci hadn't even started thinking about presents. She didn't have much holiday spirit this year.

She had to walk a few blocks from the bus stop, and she was cold by the time she got to Sunrise House. The overly-warm air inside felt good.

She got permission to see Danny, and found him sitting in the rocker by the window.

"Hello, Danny," she said.

He turned at the sound of her voice, but he just looked at her blankly. As she came closer, she saw that one of his eyes looked blank.

"It's me—Traci. Mark couldn't make it today, but he said to tell you 'hi.' "

"Traci?" He peered at her. "I don't see too well these days. It's nice of you to come over here on such a cold day."

She had brought some magazines, but she decided not to give them to Danny until she found out if he could read them. "I like cold weather," she said. "Mark and I both love to ski."

"I've never—" he began, but a fit of coughing racked his thin body. After he stopped coughing, he seemed exhausted.

"Don't you want to lie down?" Traci asked.

"No, I like it here in the sun."

"But there is no—I like the sun, too," she said quickly, her heart almost breaking because he didn't even know that there was no sun today. *Oh Danny, you're so much worse now.*

"I'm so cold all the time." He shivered and pulled his robe tighter around his neck. "My mom used to have one of those glass balls— the kind you shake and the snow whirls around in it. There was a boy inside building a snowman."

Traci nodded. "My grandma had one like that. Only it had a girl inside."

He went on as if he hadn't heard her. "I feel like that boy inside. The snow is swirling around me, and I can't get out. I'm trapped

131

inside." He looked toward Traci. "Who did you say you were?"

Traci tried not to show her shock. *He doesn't know me,* she thought. "I'm Traci Crawford. We went to grade school together. You and Mark were in the hospital at the same time."

"Mark? I don't believe I know a Mark."

"Mark Crawford. My uncle. You two played chess."

"Chess." Danny's face brightened. "I love chess. Daddy gave me a chess set." He looked around. "Where is it?" His voice was agitated. "Where is it?" He fumbled at the things on a table beside him, knocking off a pitcher of water.

At the sound of the crash, a young man hurried in. "It's okay, Danny. We'll get it cleaned right up."

"Bob! Bob, somebody took my chess set! I want it back," Danny said like a very small boy. He began to cry. "I want it back, please."

"It's right on your bed," the man said. "You were playing with it this morning."

"Oh...that's good."

The man helped Danny back to the bed. "See, it's right here."

Danny sat down on the bed and began to move the pieces around the board. He didn't seem to realize that Traci was in the room.

"I guess I'd better go," Traci whispered to the man. "Could I talk to you first?"

"I'll be right out," he said. "I just want to get Danny settled down."

Traci hurried from the room and leaned against the wall in the hallway. When the man came out, Traci asked, "What's wrong with Danny? One minute he recognized me, then he didn't seem to know either me or my uncle."

"I'm Bob, a volunteer orderly here," he said. "Come on downstairs where we can talk."

Bob didn't look much older than Mark. He offered Traci a chair in the converted office.

"You're Traci, aren't you?" he asked. "Danny has talked about you and Mark a lot. Your visits are helping him get through a bad time."

"He seems so sick now," she said. "He's terribly thin—and—and old looking."

Bob nodded. "Danny has bad days and some not so bad. Most of the time, he recognizes people, but not always."

"But why? It isn't just his eyes, is it?"

"No. His eyes are affected. But so is his brain. HIV attacks the part of the body that defends us against many unusual diseases. Danny's immune system is nearly destroyed and has allowed his brain to become infected with one of those diseases."

"Does—does everybody with AIDS get that way?" she asked, thinking of Mark.

"No. Sometimes other parts of the body are affected. It's a terrible, terrible disease," he said angrily.

"Shouldn't Danny be in a hospital?"

"Only if he needs special care. We can do most things for him right here."

"He's so cold...." Tears welled to Traci's eyes. "Can't you make him warm?"

"I know," he said sympathetically. "It's hard to see him like this. But maybe next time you visit, he'll have one of his good days. Maybe it would help if you went to one of the support groups for families and friends of people with AIDS. They meet every Tuesday night at one of the counselors' houses."

Bob looked for some papers and brochures on the desk. "Take a look at these. They tell all about the support groups."

"Thanks. I'll read them before I come back to visit."

*****

But Traci was so busy with Christmas preparations that she didn't have a chance to come back and visit Danny again until the morning of Christmas Eve.

She went over to Mark's to see if he wanted to go along and found him still in his robe. "How about driving me to Melrose? I want to buy a little present for Danny. I'm taking some cookies and fudge. Can you think of anything else?"

"We could give him the white knight from my chess set. We can always use something else."

"That's a great idea—but I know that set means a lot to you."

Mark shrugged. "It's the perfect gift."

She agreed. Danny would love it. "Will you take me to see him?"

"I'd like to, but I still have a Christmas present to finish."

"Sure, that's okay. I can take the bus."

"Why don't you ask Anthony to take you? He just got his driver's license. He'd probably like to show off."

"I hate to ask him," Traci said.

"Then I will." Mark picked up the new phone by the couch and punched in the numbers. "Anthony told me to call him if I needed anything."

Anthony not only agreed, he was there in ten minutes. Traci barely had time to find the chess piece and wrap it.

"This is really nice of you," Traci told Anthony as they were leaving. "I won't stay long at the hospice. I just want to give Danny a present."

"That's okay. I need to go to Melrose, too," he said. "I had a special gift made for Grams. I have to pick it up today."

Mark stood shivering on the porch. "Anthony, you drive carefully," he called. "Traci, tell Danny I'll see him soon."

Traci sighed. "I hope Mark's okay. He isn't shaved yet or dressed. It's not like him to just lie around the house."

"He's going through a rough time," Anthony said. "Just give him some space."

Traci gave Anthony an admiring look. "How did you get so smart so young?"

"I was born that way," he said jokingly.

Anthony did seem a lot more grown up than the other guys she knew. On the trip to Melrose, he talked about himself for the first time. His mother worked as a nurse at the local hospital. His father died of lung cancer when Anthony was seven. "That's why I'll never smoke," he said.

"I'm lucky to have my mom and dad," Traci told him. "But I wish Grandma and Grandpa Crawford were still alive. My other grandparents live in Florida. I only see them once a year, but at least I see them."

"Grams and Mom are all the family I have," Anthony said wistfully. "I've always kind of envied kids who have big family picnics and Christmases and Thanksgivings."

He grinned at Traci. "Maybe my mom will marry a man with six kids."

"What? And have to share your room?"

Anthony laughed. "I sleep on the couch in the living room. I wouldn't mind sharing a real bedroom with a couple of brothers."

The two of them talked a little about the campaign. "Have you worked up a speech for the rally?" Traci asked.

"It's about how the four grades need to work together to get what we want. There's too much arguing among the student reps. We could accomplish a lot if everybody would just work together."

Traci had to smile at his enthusiasm. "You should run for mayor or governor someday."

"Actually, I'd rather be president," he said with a grin. "Seriously, I do want to get a law degree and then go into politics."

Neither one said anything for a bit, then Anthony broke the silence. "Traci, I know you have a lot on your mind, but—would you like to go ice skating on Wednesday afternoon? I don't have to work."

Traci liked the idea. "Sure," she said. "I love to skate. You should see Mark and—Anthony, I'm so worried about him. He seems even more depressed than ever."

"Maybe it's just the Christmas season. My mom says a lot of the patients at the hospital get really sad during the holidays."

"I hope that's it."

Traci was pleased that she could be herself around Anthony. She didn't have to be careful about what she said. He always seemed to understand. She was sorry when they pulled up in front of the hospice.

"When do you want me to pick you up?" he asked.

"Give me about 45 minutes."

As she got out of the car, Traci looked up at the threatening black clouds. She'd hoped the sun would be shining for Danny today.

No one was at the desk, so Traci went on upstairs to Danny's room. He wasn't there, but she went on inside and sat in the rocker by the window.

The other bed was rumpled. And men's clothing lay on the chair beside it. Traci was glad to see that Danny had a new roommate.

She saw Danny's chess board on the bed. Maybe that meant this was one of his good days. She rocked slowly back and forth, thinking about Danny. Would his father come to visit on Christmas? she wondered.

As she set the gift on the table beside the chair, the rain began. At first, small drops spattered the window. "Sorry, Danny, no sunshine today," she said softly.

Sighing, she got up and went over to the bed. From across the room, she hadn't noticed that the chess pieces were strewn over the blanket. She idly began to pick them up and place them in their correct positions on the board. Danny would like the gift she'd brought.

At a sound at the door, she stood up. The word "Danny" was on her lips, but it was Bob, the orderly. His face looked white. "How did you get in here?" he asked sharply.

"There wasn't anybody at the desk, so I just came on up. I'm sorry, if that's against the rules."

"No, no, it's not that. Maybe we'd better go downstairs."

Fingers of ice touched Traci's neck. *Please tell me Danny's just gone home for the holidays.*

"Danny's gone back to the hospital," she said. "That's it, isn't it? He got worse and had to go back."

Bob came over and put his arm around Traci's shoulders. "I'm sorry, Traci. Danny died this morning."

"No! I brought him a present and some Christmas fudge. He was my friend, and I never—I never got to—" A terrible lump in her throat choked off her words.

"Danny had seemed to be feeling a little better," Bob said. "His father came to see him last night. Danny was looking at his chess set when he suddenly had a seizure. He never woke up after the seizure, and he died quietly and peacefully."

Traci's eyes felt hot and dry, but she didn't cry. "I should have come sooner. I should have been here."

"There is nothing you should have done or could have done," Bob told her. "This was the best way for him to go. Anyway, Danny wouldn't have recognized you. The disease ate away bit by bit until Danny was just a shell. Come on downstairs," Bob said gently.

"Do you mind if I stay in here for a few minutes?"

He hesitated. "Are you sure?"

Traci nodded. "I'll only be a minute," she said. "I never got to say good-bye."

Bob left the room, closing the door behind him.

Traci went back to the bed and slowly began to put the chess pieces back into the box. She laid the safety-pin knight aside, then got a small package from the table. She opened it and took out the white knight. "It's not like your old one, Danny, but I hope you like it."

Very carefully, she placed the knight in the old chess box and closed the lid. The sharp click sounded loud in the quiet room—so final.

Traci's throat ached from trying not to cry. She crossed to the window. Sleet was beating against the glass now. The small particles slid down the pane like icy tears.

"You'll be warm now, Danny," she whispered softly.

Twelve

TRACI stared dry-eyed through the sleet that threatened to stop the windshield wipers. The only sounds in the car were the dull roar of the heater fan, the crunch of tires on icy pavement, and the hesitant swish of the wipers.

"Are you going to be okay?" Anthony asked.

"Kids shouldn't die at sixteen!" Traci cried angrily. "People shouldn't die alone. Nobody cares!"

"But you did. And I'll bet Danny knew that."

Traci gave Anthony a grateful look. "I hope so. I sure hope so."

"It's rough to lose somebody," Anthony said quietly. "I just couldn't believe my dad was dead. I kept telling everybody he was on a trip. But when he didn't show up for my birthday, I knew."

He let out a long sigh. "It's okay to cry, you know."

Traci shook her head. "If I start, I might not be able to stop."

They didn't say much on the ride home. Anthony had to concentrate on the icy road. When they pulled into the driveway, he put his hand over Traci's. "I'm really sorry. You won't want to go ice skating Wednesday. We can go some other time."

"Thanks for taking me to the hospice. And thanks for understanding."

As Traci got out of the car, she said, "Anthony, I almost forgot. Come on in for a minute. I have a present for you."

Anthony waited in the front entry while Traci went into the family room to get his gift from under the tree. As she was giving him the box of candy and homemade cookies, Mrs. Bagley came into the hall carrying her spray can of disinfectant. She was not only wearing rubber gloves and a mask, but she also had on a long raincoat. She looked like a worker in a nuclear plant.

"Mark is upstairs." She scowled. "I'm fixing him some soup. Now, I have to wash all his dishes in bleach."

Traci was in no mood for Mrs. Bagley's paranoia about germs. *Maybe you should use paper plates,* she wanted to say.

"Mark said you've been to visit that sick boy, Danny." Mrs. Bagley began spraying around Anthony's and Traci's feet. "I thought your mother didn't want you going to see him again. I'm afraid I'm going to have to tell her."

"Oh, you don't have to tell her anything, Mrs. Bagley." Traci felt hot tears rush to her eyes. She blinked them back. "Danny died this morning."

* * * * *

On Christmas Day, Melissa came over to see Traci's presents. "I got the watch I've been wanting," Melissa said. "And a new sweater and skirt. And a bunch of other stuff. How about you?"

Traci took Melissa into the family room. She tried to sound happy as she pointed out her gifts under the tree.

"Wow, that picture of you is really beautiful."

"That's the one that got slashed at the art fair. I didn't even know Mark was doing it over," Traci said. She figured that this was the painting he'd been working on when she'd asked him to visit Danny. The only thing she'd have liked better would have been a self-portrait of Mark—in case....

Traci wished she could stop thinking of Mark dying, but the image of Danny huddled in the rocking chair haunted her. In her dream the night before, Danny's face had turned into Mark's.

"Traci? Are you okay?"

Melissa's words startled her. "What?"

"Are you all right? You looked so sad. Is it— Mark?"

"No—and yes," Traci said. "His immune system is worse. And—and Danny died yesterday." She blinked rapidly. "I'm just so scared for Mark. I feel like crying all the time. I know that won't help him, but I just don't know what to do!" The tears she'd been holding back for so long rolled down her cheeks. "Melissa, what will I do if he—if—if he dies, too?"

Melissa didn't say anything—she was just there.

Traci wiped her eyes on the sleeve of her sweater. "I'm sorry. For Mark's sake, I've been trying to be cheerful, but sometimes it all gets to me."

"Want to do something to take your mind off things?" Melissa asked.

"I don't think so." She walked Melissa to the door. They hugged each other for a long time. "Thanks for being my friend."

* * * * *

On Monday Traci went to see Mark. She found him reading the pamphlets Bob had given her. "These are great," he said. He was shaved and dressed and didn't sound the least bit depressed. "There's an article here on visualization," Mark said. "I'm supposed to imagine that a little video character is gobbling up the virus."

Traci forced a laugh. "Maybe I can visualize it eating up some of my freckles."

It's odd, Traci thought, looking at Mark's smiling face. After Danny's death, she had expected him to just give up. Instead he was acting like the old Mark again.

"Did you get some good news, Mark? You seem happier than I've seen you lately. I thought—after Danny..."

Mark shook his head slowly. "After Danny died, I knew I couldn't just lie around waiting to see if I am going to develop AIDS. I may only have a few months or a few years. Or I could have a whole lifetime. But whatever time I have left, I'm going to make the most of it."

"Mark, I'm so glad."

"Yeah, I've been a pain in the neck lately. I kept feeling as if a sword were hanging over my head and I was just waiting for it to drop. I

147

don't know how you put up with me."

Traci picked up one of the pamphlets. "This one says you have to strengthen your immune system by diet and exercise, and get rid of stress. You have to try to stay healthy until there's a cure for AIDS. And you have to have a positive attitude."

She searched through the papers until she found a list of dates for support groups. "The volunteer at the hospice mentioned the support groups. There's a meeting for HIV positive people tomorrow night at seven at the Project."

Traci continued on hurriedly so Mark wouldn't interrupt. "At the same time there's one for families and friends of people with AIDS or ARC or who test positive for HIV. That group meets in a private home, but the time is the same time as for the meeting at the Project. We could each go to one of the groups."

"I told you before—I'm not interested. I don't see what good it would do."

But this time Mark didn't seem to be so much against the idea.

"I think it would help us both," she said. "Maybe we can get Mom and Dad to come, too."

"I guess I might as well. You won't let up

until I agree. Did anyone ever tell you you're stubborn?"

"Well, that makes two of us, doesn't it?"

They took the brochures back to Traci's house. When her parents came home from the restaurant, she didn't even wait for them to take off their coats. "Mom? Dad? Mark and I have something important to ask you."

"Just let me sit down first," her father said. "I'm beat."

They all went back into the family room, and as soon as her parents were settled, she said, "Mark and I want you to come to a support group tomorrow night. He'll go to one group, and we'll go to one for families."

Traci's parents looked at each other. Finally her father said, "I don't think that's a good idea. Some of our customers might see us there."

"But the meetings are in Melrose," Mark said.

"Plenty of our customers go to Melrose," her mother said.

Traci's father suddenly got up and went over to the portrait Mark had painted of Traci and his mother. "I think it's fine for you, Mark, but not for the rest of us."

"Mom, I want to go," Traci said, knowing her mother would be more likely to say yes.

"The group meets in a private home. Who's going to know?"

Her mother looked at the pamphlets and papers on AIDS. "I just think you're getting far too involved in this."

"I want to be involved in anything that concerns Mark," Traci said.

"Your mother and I are just as concerned as you are," her father said. "But I don't think going to a support group is the answer."

"I didn't either," Mark said. "But I do think Traci should go."

"Well..." her mother said doubtfully. "You may be right. I suppose it doesn't do any good to pretend it will all go away. Alan? What do you think?"

Her father looked at Mark. "Do you really think this group will help you and Traci deal with what's happened to you?"

Mark nodded.

"All right." Traci's father gave a deep sigh. "I guess one time won't hurt. But, Traci, if you come home all upset the way you were the other day, you won't go again."

"You can't go alone," her mother put it. "I suppose I could go with you. Maybe you'd better leave some of those pamphlets for me to read."

*****

The next night, Mark drove Traci and her mother to the family and friends support group. "I'll pick you up just as soon as my meeting is over," he told them.

A woman about the age of Traci's mother invited them in. There were maybe ten people already there, sitting in a semi-circle.

"I'm Dorothy," the woman said. "We're very informal here. There are cold drinks and coffee in the kitchen." She pointed to a hallway. "The bathroom's that way. We have only two rules. No last names. And everything you hear is strictly confidential."

Traci and her mother nodded and took seats next to each other. A few more people came in. Then Dorothy, who called herself a facilitator, welcomed everyone. It was obvious that many of the people knew each other and had been coming to the group for some time.

One woman was embroidering a name on a large panel of material. She held it up for everyone to see. "This is for Michael." She swallowed several times and when she spoke, her voice was strained. "I'm getting this ready for the AIDS Quilt." She ran her fingers over the outline of a teddy bear on the fabric and gave a pained little laugh. "Mikey never went to bed without his bear."

"For those of you who are new to the group, the AIDS Quilt is a memorial for people who have died of AIDS," Dorothy explained. "Next week there's going to be a ceremony displaying the panels made in our area. If you're interested, help yourselves to the brochures on the table by the door."

The woman with the quilt panel held it to her face as if it were a baby's blanket. "I used to cry every time something reminded me of Michael." Her voice wavered. "Making the quilt has helped me say good-bye."

Touched by the woman's grief, nobody spoke for a minute. "Mary, why don't you start?" the facilitator finally said to a woman who looked about fifty. "You haven't been here for several weeks. How is Craig doing?"

"Not well at all. He's in the hospital. Pneumocystis pneumonia again." Her eyes glittered with tears. "I—I don't see how he can last much longer."

They went around the room, each person telling a little bit about their problems. Just talking about it with sympathetic listeners seemed to help. One man was so angry he could hardly speak. A doctor had refused to treat his son.

One of the women spoke up. "Hang onto the

anger. It'll help you have the strength and energy to get through this thing we're all facing."

For the first time Dorothy gave some specific suggestions. "Just don't bottle up anger. Focus it—do something constructive with it. Write letters to the government for more help. Act as a volunteer. Turn the anger into a positive force."

Traci hoped Mark was getting some help from his group.

One man was having trouble with insurance. His insurance company had tried to get out of paying a hospital bill. Different people in the group offered suggestions and told him where to get help. Others talked about their feelings, their pain, their anger. Then it was Traci's turn. Suddenly she was nervous. She almost wished she hadn't come to the meeting. She glanced at her mother.

Dorothy smiled sympathetically. "If you don't want to talk, that's all right. But if you have a problem, maybe we can help."

Traci's mother nodded. "Go ahead, honey."

"My problems seem so silly after hearing what everybody else is going through," Traci said.

"The first time I came here, I was too ashamed to admit that my daughter had

153

AIDS," one woman said to Traci. "I told everybody she had leukemia. Now, that's pretty silly."

Traci glanced at her mother. "I haven't told anybody this," Traci said. "I know I can't get HIV from a drinking glass. But sometimes I won't even pick up Mark's glass. And after he's used a spoon or something, I have to force myself not to go wash it in bleach like our housekeeper does."

"It's a natural reaction," a man said. "There's been so much misinformation about AIDS. I wouldn't even hug my son." His Adam's apple went up and down as he blinked back tears. "Now it's too late."

One woman who looked older than the rest talked about her grandson. "I practically raised Gary when he was little." She smiled, almost too herself. "He was such an adorable baby. And he was so good. He never cried. He and I were always close. Sometimes I'd forget that he wasn't my son. You know what he did for my seventieth birthday?"

The woman was looking directly at Traci, so Traci shook her head.

"He took off work and flew two hundred miles so he'd get to my apartment at noon. He came walking in with one long-stemmed rose, a feast of piping hot Chinese food—all my favorite dishes, and a box of candy. He hugged me and said, 'I love you, Granny.' " The woman smiled at Traci and then went on... "I didn't have the heart to tell him the almond toffee was impossible to eat with dentures.

"Last month he called me and said could I come to see him. He was in the hospital, all hooked up to tubes and machines. He was so thin I hardly recognized him. 'Hi, Granny,' he said. His voice was so weak, I had to bend down to hear him."

The woman's eyes swam with tears. "I held my baby. I didn't care about the tubes and machines. I screamed at God. *Why Gary? How can You be so cruel?*

" 'It's all right,' Gary told me. 'I can let loose now that you're here.' " The woman's chin trembled and she bit her lower lip.

" 'I—love—you—Granny,' he whispered. Oh, dear God, I miss him so much!"

Thirteen

AS Traci and her mother left the support group, Traci noticed that her mother's eyes were red. Her own throat was still too tight to say anything. She stopped to pick up a brochure about the memorial quilt. Maybe she and Mark could make one for Danny.

Mark was waiting for them out front. He, too, was solemn. Nobody said anything for a few minutes. Finally, Mark cleared his throat. "Well, how was your group?"

"I'm drained from all the pain and heartache those people are feeling," Traci's mother said softly. "I've never seen so much courage. I'm glad I came, Mark. How about you?"

"I don't feel as sorry for myself anymore," Mark said. "I found out I wasn't the only one feeling depressed and wondering if I was going crazy or something. I can't really say much about the group, because everything is supposed to be kept confidential."

"They stressed that in our group, too," Traci said.

"Some people have it really rough," Mark went on. "Their families have totally rejected them."

"And yet, there was one mother in our group who hadn't been out of the house for two months until tonight," Traci said. "She's been taking care of her eleven-year-old son night and day."

"Do you mind if we drive past the city park?" Mark asked.

"It's fine with me," Traci's mother said. "I don't want to go home just yet, anyway. I'm all wrung out."

"What's in the park?" Traci wanted to know.

"One of the guys at the group said he was living there. He was kicked out of his apartment. A couple of other people said they'd lost their jobs. They have no money, no families, no insurance. They're afraid they might have to live in the park or in their cars."

"That's awful!" Traci's mother said.

Mark drove slowly past the large park by the river. Traci saw people bundled up in blankets and newspapers, or huddled under a bush.

"I wonder how many people with AIDS will

end up here." Mark hit the steering wheel with his fist. "I just feel as if I ought to do something!"

"I suppose we could distribute food from the restaurant," Traci's mother said. "But they can probably get meals from the church missions. I just don't understand why Melrose isn't doing something about it. Doesn't anybody care?"

"The AIDS Project has a food bank that you could give to. They have volunteers who distribute the food, but they need more help and more donations. The problem is that until this ugly disease touches people personally, nobody wants to get involved," Mark said. "It won't be long, though, before almost everyone will be touched—they'll all know someone who has died of AIDS." Mark said sadly.

No one said much on the drive back to Weston. They all seemed lost in their own thoughts. At the house, Traci and her mother started to get out of the car.

"Wait, Linda," Mark said. "Can we talk a minute? You and Traci both."

"Mark, is something wrong?" Traci's mother asked quickly. Traci noticed that he ignored the question. He hadn't told her mom and dad what was happening to his immune system.

"On the way home I was thinking. There is

something we can do to help people with AIDS, that is, if you and Alan will agree."

"After tonight, I'm not too likely to say no," Traci's mother said.

"What is it?" Traci asked. "I want to help, too."

"Well, you know the Melrose Hospice Association has been trying to find a suitable house. I was thinking—how about if we donate the old place? It's plenty large enough. It's not in a residential zone anymore."

"I'm not against the idea. I don't think that house will ever sell. But what about you, Mark? Where would you live?"

"I could keep my own room, and volunteer to help. I'd still be able to paint."

"If you're feeling better, I'd think that you'd want to get a job or go to art school."

Mark spun the steering wheel several times, then turned to Traci's mother. "There's something I've been meaning to tell you and Alan. The last check of my T cells showed that my immune system is quite suppressed. The doctor wants me to start taking AZT. It's a drug that's seemed to help some people to feel better and live longer. So who knows, I may be needing hospice care before long myself."

"Oh, Mark, I'm so sorry," Traci's mother said. "But you mustn't give up hope."

"I haven't. And I'm doing everything I can to help myself—eating right, exercising, trying to have a positive attitude. I've even had some instruction in meditation that's helping."

"That sounds good. Just don't let some of these unscrupulous people get to you. I was reading about how much money is spent on quack cures."

Traci looked at her mother in surprise. She had actually been reading about AIDS.

"Don't worry," Mark assured her. "I'll be careful. So, what do you think about the house?" he asked.

"I think it's a fine idea. Alan has been pretty upset about all the reactions to a hospice. I think he'll agree."

"I'll get Melissa and Anthony to volunteer," Traci said. "We can do errands and write letters and things like that. Did you read about the Teen-AIDS Hotline? Maybe we could start one."

"I'm lucky to have you guys," Mark said. "Thanks for going tonight, Linda."

"The group certainly gave me plenty to think about," she said.

"Mark, I'll be over tomorrow," Traci said. "I want you to help me with an idea I've got. It's something for Danny."

*****

The next morning Traci hurried over to the old house. She showed Mark the article about the memorial quilt. "It's called the Names Project Quilt. 'The memorial quilt with over 2,000 panels was first unfolded in Washington, D.C.,' " she read aloud. " 'It's a symbol of love and compassion.' "

"I remember seeing it on TV," Mark said. "It was huge."

"Well, it's a lot bigger now. It would cover several football fields." Traci's eyes felt hot with tears. "Every panel is for somebody who has died of AIDS."

"And you want us to make one for Danny? I think it's a great idea."

"We don't have much time to get it into the local display in Wakefield."

"So we'll work fast," Mark said.

"This article tells how to make one. The panels measure three feet by six feet. You could paint Danny's name and a big chess knight on it. How about Danny 'the Squeaker?' That's what his dad used to call him."

"Well, what are we waiting for? Let's go buy some material and get started."

They drove to the fabric store, and Traci found a piece of heavy yellow cloth. "Danny always wanted to be warm," she told Mark. "This bright yellow makes me think of the sun."

Mark bought red and black textile paint, and they hurried back to the old house. They worked in silence. Maybe it was only a very small thing to do, but Traci felt it was a way to say good-bye to Danny.

As Mark painted the chess knight, Traci's throat tightened. She remembered Danny and Mark playing together. She was close to tears, but this was no time to cry.

When they finished the quilt panel, Mark said, "I'll run this over to Wakefield. Then tomorrow night we can go to the ceremony."

Traci ran her fingers over the material, then glanced at Mark. *Will I be making a memorial quilt for you some day?* Angry with herself for being so pessimistic, she dropped the panel. *I have to stop thinking that way,* she thought.

The next evening she and Mark drove over to Wakefield where the panels would be displayed for a few days before they were added to the National AIDS Quilt. Traci had asked her parents to come with them, but they said they had too many holiday banquets. They couldn't get away.

When Mark and Traci arrived at the huge auditorium, Mark started scanning the crowd.

"Are you expecting someone?" Traci asked. "Are Mom and Dad coming after all?"

"Don't be upset, Traci, but I did something without asking you. I asked Danny's dad to meet us here. I told him we'd made a panel for Danny."

"If he didn't care enough to see Danny alive, why would he want to see the panel?"

"Don't judge him," Mark said. "He may be feeling awful."

Mark's right, she thought. She felt sorry for Mr. Walsh because he'd lost both his wife and now Danny. But it was hard to forgive him.

She and Mark waited by the front entrance. When everyone else had gone inside, Traci said, "He isn't going to show up. Let's go on in. We're going to miss the ceremony."

"Just give him five more minutes."

Finally, Mr. Walsh came hurrying up. He was still dressed in his work clothes. "I'm sorry I'm late," he said breathlessly. "There was an accident on the highway, and I was late getting back from my truck run."

He and Mark shook hands. "I'm glad you could make it. Do you remember Traci?" Mark asked, turning to her.

"Of course, I do. I remember you used to eat a lot of peanut butter cookies."

"Danny's mom made great cookies," Traci

said. It was hard to know what to say. "I—I was really sorry to hear about Mrs. Walsh."

As if he didn't want to talk about his wife, Mr. Walsh said quickly, "Maybe we should go in." Then he paused and looked at Mark and Traci. "But before we do, though, I—uh—I want to thank you both for going to see Danny."

As he said Danny's name, Mr. Walsh choked a little. "I really appreciate your telling me about the quilt panel you made."

"You don't have to thank us," Traci said. "We did it because we wanted to. He was our friend."

Traci quickly hurried up the steps to the auditorium. By the time they got inside and found some seats, the guest speaker was just finishing.

"...Life is sacred and to be honored—that is the message of the quilt."

The lights dimmed and a spotlight shone on the far wall. There was a sound of cymbals in the background as the first panels unfolded.

Silence fell over the huge auditorium as a group of men and women dressed all in white stood in a circle. In perfect cadence they took turns reading the names of all the people in the area who had died of AIDS. A rush of feeling overwhelmed Traci, and she reached for Mark's hand.

The spotlight rested on each section of quilt as it unfurled. As the names went on and on and on, Traci felt a chill go over her. So many had died.

Traci had thought it was odd that she knew two people with the virus. But after hearing all the names of people who had died from AIDS in just this local area, it didn't seem so odd anymore. Before, the thousands of people she'd read about were only numbers. But the panels made her realize that every number had a name—the name of someone's brother or friend or father or child. *Or uncle.*

When the last name was read, the large hall was silent, except for the sound of someone sobbing.

The lights came up. Volunteers in white unfolded quilt sections of eight panels each, until the floor was covered. Suddenly, every person in the room reached out to take the hand of the one next to him. With tears in her eyes, Traci reached out to Mark. He took her hand and gave it a little squeeze.

She turned to take the hand of the person on her other side, forgetting it was Danny's father. She hesitated for a second, then his large hand enveloped hers. As their arms raised high, a wave of love and hope flooded through her. People did care, after all.

The host announced that everyone could now view the panels. Traci gripped Mark's hand, and they began to walk on the runways between the rows of panels, looking for the one they'd made for Danny. Mr. Walsh followed.

Some panels were made of faded jeans, some had small objects attached to them. Others had messages painted on them. One just said, GOOD-BYE, DAD.

Traci glanced up at Mark. His face was pale and drawn as if in pain. Was he thinking—will there be one of these panels for me some day soon?

"There are so many," he whispered, almost to himself. "So many."

The haunting music of a flute floated through the huge auditorium. Over in the corner, sitting cross-legged in front of a panel, a young man played softly.

When they had looked at the last panel without finding Danny's, Traci said, "I don't understand. Why isn't it here?"

"I'm sorry, Mr. Walsh. Maybe it's someplace else," Mark said. "I'll go ask one of the volunteers."

Traci and Mr. Walsh stood in awkward silence until Mark returned. "They didn't get

Danny's panel in time to sew it together with seven others. It's in another room," Mark said. "We can go look at it."

In a large basement room, a volunteer found Danny's panel for them and spread it out on the floor.

Danny's father sank to his knees in front of the piece of cloth. He looked up at Mark and Traci. "It's beautiful," he said, his eyes brimming with tears. He touched the painted knight. "Danny liked to play chess. Even after he lost one of the pieces, he hung onto the old set I gave him."

Seeing the pain on Mr. Walsh's face, Traci's heart went out to him. She wanted to cry for him, for Danny, for all the people who had died of AIDS. She reached out to touch Mr. Walsh's shoulder, wishing there was some way to give him comfort.

"Danny, I came to the hospice to tell you I found us a nice apartment," he said, still staring at the panel. "I bought a Christmas tree and an angel for the top just like the one we used to have. I haven't been much of a father since your mom died. But I just want you to know—" His voice cracked. "I love you, son."

Mr. Walsh got slowly to his feet. Almost in a whisper, he said, "So long, Squeaker."

Fourteen

EVERY New Year's Eve the restaurant put on a huge party. One banquet room was set aside for a teen party with a jukebox for dancing, video games, and plenty of food. The main dining room was turned into a ballroom for the adults.

On Saturday, when Traci and Melissa arrived at the restaurant to help, Traci's father told her to help Anthony set up the teen room. A few people were still eating dinner in the main dining room, which was decorated with balloons and lights. Traci was amused to see that her dad had let Anthony put up several of his posters.

At nine o'clock, the tables would come down, and the dining room would become a ballroom. A five-piece band would play dance music for the adults.

At nine o'clock, the crowd began to arrive.

Business hadn't appeared to have suffered because of Mark's illness. Soon the teen room was full. Most of the kids were eighth, ninth, and tenth graders. The older kids usually went to private parties. Traci noticed that several kids who had refused to come to the Halloween party were there. Nobody snubbed her, but nobody asked her to dance, either.

When Anthony took his break, he came over to see Traci. "How's it going?" he asked loudly, trying to make himself heard over the rock and roll music. "Are the kids avoiding you?"

"No, not really. Maybe you're right. Maybe they are getting used to the idea."

"Want to dance?" Anthony asked.

"If you don't mind being seen with me."

"Don't be dumb," he said, and led her out on the crowded floor.

At eleven, Anthony had to leave to help set up the midnight supper. A little later on all the kids came out to the main room. Traci and Melissa passed out hats and noisemakers.

The band was playing something slow when Traci saw Mark come in. As he pushed his way through the crowd, she noticed people draw back from him. She was standing near the band, but she could still hear people muttering, "What's he doing here?" and, "I'm not staying in the same room with Mark Crawford!"

Traci knew by Mark's white, grim face that he had heard the remarks, too.

A few couples headed for the coat room. Traci felt her face turn hot with anger. How could people be so rude, so uncaring?

More and more people were leaving. When Traci heard a man say, "We don't need his kind in Weston. Why don't they quarantine him?" she couldn't bear it anymore. She hesitated, hating to make a scene. Then she stepped up onto the little raised platform and asked the band to stop playing. She told the drummer to get the crowd's attention.

Traci's parents rushed to her side. "What's going on?" her father wanted to know. "Why is everyone leaving?"

Instead of answering, Traci pulled the microphone close. "Don't anybody take another step out of here," she said, shocked by her own words.

"Traci, get down here," her father hissed.

"Not yet, Dad. Not until I say something."

Mark had joined her parents. "Traci, don't do this," he said. "It's not worth it." He stepped up onto the stage and held up his hand. "I'm Mark Crawford. I know you're all afraid of getting the AIDS virus from me. I saw a poster today. It said, 'Fear is in the air. AIDS is not.'"

The crowd stood silent. Nobody was leaving.

"You can't get the virus by touching me, but I just wanted you to know that you don't need to leave the party. It was a mistake for me to come here."

A rumble went through the crowd. "It was a mistake for you to stay in Weston!" a man shouted.

"Get out of here, get out of our town!" another yelled.

Mark started to step down, but Traci grabbed his arm. "No! I can't keep quiet any longer." She lifted the microphone off the stand and moved close to the edge of the stage.

"What's the matter with all of you?" she said, trying to control her anger. "What's happened to this town? My Grandpa Crawford used to say that Weston was the friendliest town in the country. He said people used to help each other when they were in trouble."

Traci took a deep breath. "Well, now my uncle Mark is in trouble. He got the HIV virus from getting a blood transfusion after a serious accident. He might even have AIDS now. It could happen to anybody. It could happen to one of you. He told you that you can't get AIDS by touching him. And if you people would take the time to read about the subject, you wouldn't act this way."

Traci reached out, took Mark's hands, and pulled him toward her. She stood on tiptoe and kissed him on the cheek. "He wouldn't let me do that if he thought it was dangerous."

"What do you know about it?" a woman called out. "You're not a doctor."

"No, I'm just a kid, and maybe I don't know much. But I've read a lot of articles and what the Surgeon General has to say about AIDS. And I know I love my uncle Mark, and I can't bear to see him hurt."

Traci's father stepped up onto the stage next to Mark and took the mike. "What is it they say—out of the mouth of babes comes truth. I've been reacting the same as all of you. I wouldn't let Mark work here or even come to the restaurant, because I was afraid I'd lose all of you as customers. I'm ashamed to say it, but I've been afraid to shake my brother's hand or touch him since I learned he had the virus."

Traci watched as her father turned and started to shake Mark's hand. But instead, he drew Mark into his arms and held him close for a long moment. Traci heard him whisper, "Forgive me, little brother."

Traci's mother took the mike. "If you folks still want to leave, that's your privilege. We hope you'll come back, but we want you to know that Mark is welcome here anytime."

Traci's eyes swam with tears. She was so proud of her parents that she was about to burst.

Melissa and Anthony rushed up to Traci. "You were great," Melissa said.

"You're getting pretty good at these speeches," Anthony said, grinning.

"I was so mad I didn't even think about what I was going to say. It just came out."

Traci's father put his arm around her. "For a few minutes there, I thought you'd lost your mind."

"Maybe I shouldn't have spoken out," Traci said. "You might lose a lot of business."

Traci's mother looked around. "I don't see very many people leaving. Anyway, honey, I'm proud of you."

Anthony's mother pushed his grandmother's wheelchair through the crowd. Mrs. Evans patted Traci's hand. "Good for you, child. This town needed to be shaken up a bit."

Leonard Backus, the editor of the Weston Journal, came up and spoke to Traci. "Well, young woman, you've given me the subject of my New Year's editorial." He nodded toward one of Anthony's posters. "You should be running for a school office. If I were in high school, you'd get my vote."

Traci was a little embarrassed by all the attention, but she felt wonderful.

Traci's dad motioned to the band. As they began to play "Auld Lang Syne," he called. "It's twelve o'clock! Happy New Year!"

"May I have this dance, Miss Crawford?" Mark asked. As they moved out onto the floor and began to dance, people drew aside—but not as though they were trying to avoid Mark.

Traci looked up at Mark. "I was really surprised to see you here after the way Mom and Dad have acted."

"Linda asked me to come tonight. Your mom has changed her thinking since she started learning about AIDS. She's even got Mrs. Bagley reading articles on the subject."

Traci laughed. "I'm glad," she said. "Now, we're a family again."

"Happy New Year, squirt."

"Oh, Mark, I hope so. Maybe this will be the year they discover a cure for AIDS."

Hugging her, Mark replied, "We can only hope."

Traci closed her eyes, hugging Mark tighter.

Please, God, don't let it come too late for Mark.

About the Author

ALIDA E. YOUNG lives with her husband in the high desert of Southern California. When she's writing a story, she remembers her experience in little theater. She puts herself into the shoes of a character the way an actor does. She tries to feel all the pain and hurt and all the joy and fun that the characters go through. When she's doing a book that requires research, she talks to experts. "Everyone is so helpful," she says. "They go out of their way to help."

Other books by Alida E. Young include *Why Am I Too Young?*, *What's Wrong With Daddy?*, *I'll Be Seeing You*, and *Megan the Klutz*.